It Wasn't So Strange After All

José Soler

For Brenda and Phil,

I hope you enjoy this book!

Happy travels!!

ISBN: 978-84-09-266674-6

For Eileen

It has been nine days since I received Michele's letter—an actual letter. Who writes them anymore? During this time, I've lost one love and gained a new one. That is sometimes the way the world works.

When I opened the mailbox, I didn't know what I was about to lose or gain, or for that matter, that I'd soon be flying over the Atlantic to the United States. It was seemingly a typical Wednesday. As usual, I'd met François for coffee and had put up with another of his lectures about how if I never went out and got my act together, I'd be left on the shelf. I found Michele's letter among the junk mail. It looked like nothing special—just a rectangular, ivory envelope. Only its San Francisco postmark gave it any hint of exotic mystery. I knew that tearing it open would be like opening Pandora's box. What could Michele possibly want after two years of silence?

I made my way up the steps, caressing the envelope as I took each step, feeling her skin on the rough paper. If it was a question of picking up where we had left off, in that hotel room in Barcelona with the gorgeous views down the plane tree-lined avenue, she could just count me out. It would be far wiser to put her letter away in a drawer and open it some other time, maybe on one of those rainy afternoons that left me craving love, even her intense and overwhelming kind.

"You have feelings for her too; you still love her."

"Just give me a break, will you!" My damn conscience.

In the apartment, I went straight into the kitchen and opened the trash bin under the sink to toss the flyers for the new avocado and bacon pizzas. A slightly unpleasant smell stopped me in my tracks. How could I throw away her letter without reading it? Was I nuts? Nobody deserved to have their words discarded with orange peel and chicken bones, not Michele, not even Michele, definitely not *my* Michele.

I tore open the letter so impatiently that it gave me a paper cut. I smiled for the last time that day as I caught a glimpse of her scrawled handwriting.

> *Bonjour,* André,
>
> How is everything, sweetheart? Still in search of your long-deserved happiness? I hope this letter finds its way to you at your usual Strasbourg address and that it finds you well. Forgive me for writing to you in English, but I must confess that I haven't kept my promise to learn French. *Voilà.* There just hasn't been enough time, busy as I have been getting my life in order. I imagine that Christine is all grown up now. Oh, what I'd give to be fifteen again! I can just picture her, charming and spirited. Does she have a boyfriend or perhaps a special someone?
>
> I didn't know whether to write. I was worried that it might spoil your memories of me. But here I am at a place where I simply cannot put it off any longer. I have missed you. I miss you still. I don't know whether to talk in the past or present tense. How foolish of me. I treasured feeling you by my side despite knowing—you made it clear from the very beginning—where the line was drawn and that it could not be crossed. Lines, walls, borders—all nonsense. I was delighted to accept your terms, believing as I did that life wouldn't be offering me any more gifts. I guess we never know what life will bring our way, do we? As it turns out, this morning I decided to go for a walk. It was around 11:00. I usually leave earlier because, as you know, my

pale Irish skin can't take the midday sun. Today I was too tired when I got up, and it took me quite a while to find the energy and courage to head out. So it was a short walk. It was one of those glorious winter days that you like so much. Clear. Bright. If I reached out, I could almost touch Alcatraz with my fingertips. I walked down my street. When I got to the corner with Vallejo, I stopped to catch my breath. There's a wooden bench there, under a maple tree, where I often sit for a while. I look out over the bustling city, read the lovers' names etched with penknives into the slats of the bench and into the tree trunk, and think. It is so steep that even the fog struggles up the hill. Quite often on misty days, the bench, the maple tree, and the yellow trash bin surrounded by a little patch of grass are marooned, emerging like a tiny island in the sea of clouds stretching across the Bay.

It's as close as it gets to being in Heaven!

Sometimes, there is already someone sitting there. If that's the case, we chat. You'd never believe the things people tell me. How come it's easier to open up to a stranger? Today there was nobody to talk to. Suddenly, there you were, sitting by my side. I swear André, you were so real that I thought I was the ghost. You were looking at me with your tawny eyes, holding out your hands to me, palms up. The long life line cut across them like a slap in my face. I could see the waves reflected in your pupils. They rose and fell and surged. It made no sense; the ocean is way too far below. I closed my eyes for a second and felt a drop of seawater rolling down my cheek to the corner of my mouth. I wanted to tell you that it tasted of you, but when I opened my eyes you had disappeared, leaving just a hint of your smile in the air. This has happened to me more than once. You are there in my imagination, and when I want to reach out to touch you, the mirage vanishes, and I am left alone again.

You were always a longing, so I shouldn't be surprised. Do you remember the day we met? The sky was the same blue color as today, but it got cloudier by the hour with those round, white clouds sprouting from behind the hills, looking like marshmallow skewers. They were an omen. Little by little, the clouds curled and turned gray, their plumes still blond in the dying morning light. Constable couldn't have painted a more beautiful sky. Do you remember? Tell me you haven't forgotten their patchy, hurried shadows scattered over the vineyards of Marlenheim. Tell me you haven't forgotten me.

I still love you. There, I've said it. How easy it is to tell you, even today when I was trying to hold back. At first I was a little scared of how natural it was for me to love you. God, do I sound pathetic—an old woman talking about love to a man who doesn't want to see her again. I don't care. We "women of a certain age" say whatever we please. I feel old, André, inside and out. I never thought I'd say such a thing.

My friend Angie has agreed to keep this letter and send it to you when the time comes. She knows everything. Angie is as generous as ever. She is the purest person I have ever met.

One more thing.

Go see John. He should know he is not alone in the world. You don't need to tell him about the decrepit Michele, although I suppose it will be, to a certain extent, inevitable. His full name is John Patten. He lives at Number 4 Oak Terrace in Chatham, New Jersey. It is very close to New York. I am enclosing a check that will comfortably finance your travel expenses. I will take care of everything so that you will have no problem cashing it, even under the circumstances. And that's it, my prince. Be happy. Enjoy. Fly away. Remember me from time to time, and if one day you come to San Francisco, look for me at the bench on Vallejo Street. I will wait for you in the fog, under the maple tree.

Yours always,
Michele

I folded the pages and rested them on my chest. Dead. It could not be. Michele was not the kind of person who died.

I read the letter again. I jumped from line to line like from car to car on a moving train. Where did it say it? I looked for the words "death," "pain," and "illness." Nothing. And yet there was no doubt. Michele was dying. Very likely, she had already died.

I got up from the sofa and opened the window. I stepped out onto the balcony. How was it possible for people to walk along the boulevard just as if Michele were still alive? How dare the wind blow the same and the leaves continue to grow as if this were still the very same Spring? I was angry because I would never again see her tiny blue eyes—those eyes round like buttons—nor would I feel her rough skin on my skin again. I was mad at the world. At myself. But above all, I was mad at her. Dying was completely her fault.

I didn't think about Michele's request until much later. Go see John. Just like that. Go see the son she gave up for adoption. What was I supposed to do—knock on his door and tell him point blank that he had a brother and worse, that he had a mother? For Christ's sake!

I imagined the scene. It was tragicomical.

"Hi John. Sorry to break into your life. I was bored in France so I came all the way to America just to tell you that your biological mother … Ah, you didn't know that. Really? Well, I'm telling you now. Who am I? It doesn't matter, but, by the way, since I am at it, you have a brother as well. A mother and a brother for the same price. I'm leaving now. Have a good day!"

What she had asked me to do just wasn't fair. She had four decades to tell him herself.

Besides, I barely knew anything about John, other than he had been an unexpected baby, the result of a youthful love affair. He was born a few months before me on another continent, at a time when being an unwed mother was pretty much unthinkable. Michele had told me about him on the phone, desperately, the last minute of the last day we spent in Barcelona—too late in the game for me to give him an identity. Until Michele had resurrected him in her letter, the only mental image I had of him was that of a baby leaving the delivery room wrapped in a hospital blanket on his way to meeting his new family. Who knew what he would be like now.

As for his surprise brother, I had at least seen an old, yellowed Polaroid from when he was a kid. I saw it on the day Michele and I met, the day with the clouds "with blond plumes." Only Michele talks—talked—like that. I would just have said "clouds" whether they were gray or blackish. The boy was probably about six years old when the picture was taken—a tall and thin kid in shorts riding a bicycle in front of a yellow house. I struggled to bring those photo images back—proud smile and straight, dark hair falling in bangs over his eyes. Michele was not very chatty about this other "legitimate" son either. Now, after New York, I know the reason. She called him Dawson.

Dawson and John. John and Dawson. Two perfect strangers. Two shadows in Michele's past and, in a way, each one the shadow of the other. It was almost as if Michele had lived surrounded by ghosts and when facing death she had sent them to me in the mail.

To prevent these ghosts from eating me up, I returned the sheets to the envelope and, of all things, I began to rearrange my closet. I think I was in shock. I took out my summer clothes and put the winter ones away. I left out a couple of sweaters because it can still get cool in May. I filled three garbage bags with clothes and one sports bag with old shoes. When I came across the blue shirt Michele had given me in Buenos Aires, I had to stop and sit on my bed. I spent a long time in limbo where time came and went capriciously, and past and present got mixed up until my back started to hurt. I laid on my bedspread to cry over your loss.

Nine days have passed since I received your letter, Michele. I lay on the same mattress again, my empty suitcase at the foot of the bed, my passport somewhere around—I hope. I see today, like then, how the fading light coming in through the window turns the air a graphite gray. But it smells different. It must be the smell of the clean truth clinging stubbornly to my sheets. Now I know more but not everything. Despite how crazy it may seem, I am going to answer your letter. I just have to—need to. That will be tomorrow, once I've had the chance to rest from my trip to New York.

In the meantime, until I fall asleep, I hope to find in the gloom of my room the sheltered haven where I can anchor the memories of this story I lived—we lived—at times beautiful, always strange.

I know, Michele, that you wouldn't agree with this. You wouldn't find it strange at all. Too bad. It's me who is recalling it. This is my story, but it is for you.

MICHELE

One could say that everything started by chance. At first, Michele was imposed on me. Then I got carried away. There was a time when I was the one seeking her company. I can't believe how fast the calendar pages have fallen, one after the other, like dry leaves. But I would be lying if I said that it seems like yesterday when I heard her voice for the first time because all we lived couldn't fit in one single day, just as the sea itself doesn't fit in just one conch shell—only its echo.

In that arbitrary time measured by watches, it was four years ago. Her voice came from the top of the stairs where the management offices were located. She was talking with Picard, our managing director. I knew from the start it had to be someone important because Picard used an informal tone he only dusted off when he felt outclassed. They were speaking in English. Boy, he had an accent!

"And down here we have accounting, sales, and export, Michele."

"Lovely," she said.

Love-ly, to be exact. She divided the two syllables in such a way that the "ly" arrived much later, when one had already felt her love fully. "Lovely." Love as an adjective. Michele and love were joined together from the first minute.

I turned around on my swivel chair. Our eyes met instantly. In her gaze, I saw complacency and pleasure, without a hint of pretense. Looking back, I might have continued to stick to the report I was reading on wine consumption trends in the Chinese market. Michele could have been little more than a foreign voice floating in the air for a short moment, like an exotic woman's perfume—a silky voice that had not yet spoken to me. My life would have remained exactly the same if I had not seen her go down the steps in a light zigzag, always one step ahead of Picard, her back so straight and her forehead so high that she looked like a chanteuse accustomed to making the descent of the stairs her big opening act.

I have seen many people go down those steps: managers, sales reps, administrative assistants, various guests, cleaning staff, even children during Family Day, but she was so unique that you only had to see her once to notice. I thought she was in her mid-fifties. It turned out she was quite a few years older.

Michele. I'd never forget her name.

"Let me introduce you to Mrs. Keller," Picard said. "She has come all the way from America to see us. Her brother runs *Wines of the World* magazine."

"Monsieur Broussard. Export representative. Charmed to meet you," I said.

It really bothered me to introduce myself with such a title. In my opinion, "representative" is an empty word, but in the five years I'd been there—and even now that I am on my way to my tenth anniversary—it's been impossible to replace it with another. I tried "manager" but couldn't accept "junior manager." It seemed offensive after so many years with the firm. Besides, there's no senior manager that I know of, other than maybe Picard himself, who seems to accumulate titles. Rumor has it that he even bought a barony of some lost village in Italy. Anyway, since I've just been given four boxes with five hundred business cards in each one, I guess in the short term nothing will change. Monday through Friday from 9:00 to 5:00, I'm André Broussard, export representative at Junot Cellars. The problem when I met Michele was knowing who I was the rest of the time.

I have tried to relive that first moment with Michele many times. It has always proven to be a useless effort. Whenever I remember the meeting, I just reinvent it. When she greeted me, she left her hand floating in the air at the height of my chest, like an old lady's white handkerchief. I vacillated between shaking her hand or kissing it and ended up taking it between my two hands, like a sandwich, and making the most ridiculous bow, genuflection and all. You would have thought I was in the presence of the Pope himself. Now I laugh at it, but then I felt awkward and totally out of place. I wish I could say this was an isolated feeling. François calls it my "funny pathos." He loves it. I hate it. When I looked up after my bow, Michele was two steps above staring at me with a satisfied expression, as if she knew she'd won the first round. A more careful look revealed the cautious twitching of her pupils. That to me indicated a ridiculous fear.

What possible danger could someone like me pose to her?

She smiled, accentuating the dichotomy between her suspicious eyes and the warm arch of her lips. I never got used to Michele's ability to show two different feelings, no matter how irreconcilable, at the same time. But she was like that—a beautiful drop of amber with a mosquito inside.

It didn't take Picard a minute to ask me if I was working on something urgent.

"Michele would love to visit Fort Schoenenbourg," he said.

That's how I was dragged into being her guide. That's the way our story started.

Michele had a driver. Armand was about thirty-five with prominent nose and cheekbones. His hair was slicked back so that nothing competed with his powerful gray eyes. All in all, he had that sunbathed Armani look that makes you feel you are dressed by

H&M. I spoke to him to discuss the route while Michele said goodbye to Picard at the entrance to the building.

"From here to Strasbourg, it's half an hour. How much longer do you calculate to Fort Schoenenbourg?"

He typed it into his browser with his big, strong hands. A black leather bracelet loomed under his shirt sleeve.

"That's in Hunspach," he said. "Seventy-five kilometers in total. If we leave Marlenheim now, we can be there in an hour."

Michele started to head our way, accompanied by Picard. The wind lifted her skirt. She still had beautiful legs.

"Perfect. I'll sit in the back with her, okay?" I said. "What is she like?"

"I've only been with her for two days. All right, I guess. Yes, she's fine."

Initially, it looked like it was going to be a normal trip. The first few minutes, we talked about her brother and *Wines of the World* magazine before moving on to other aspects of the wine industry. I told her about the growing interest of the Chinese in wine and how challenging it was for us to promote our white Alsatian wines in a market dominated by the Bordeaux reds and the sparkling wines of Champagne. I was just repeating what I had been reading. Michele looked distracted and generally disinterested. At one point, she interrupted me.

"Tell me, André, are you married?"

I looked at the rearview mirror and saw Armand forming a smile.

"I was."

"And? Tell me about her. What is her name?"

"Samantha."

"Like the witch in *Bewitched*," she said. Then she wrinkled her nose very strangely. "But you are way too young to know who I'm talking about."

"What exactly would you like to know?"

"Everything. I want to know everything."

I stayed quiet for a while. I didn't know where to start.

"How did you meet?" she asked.

"At my cousin Monique's wedding. The typical story of a wedding that leads to another."

I looked for Armand in the mirror again. He was focused on the road. He really was very handsome.

Talking with Michele forced me to dust off some memories that I had safely stored in a part of my brain I usually didn't travel through. Samantha and my cousin were friends, and we were seated at the same table. We were about the same age, twenty-three for her and twenty-four for me. I immediately liked her shy and fragile air. She was a sweet girl. With her bare shoulders wrapped in tulle, I thought she was a delicious *éclair* who would let itself be eaten little by little—an updated Grace Kelly. Almost at the end of the party, the wind rose in the garden of the château where my cousin held her reception. I thought Samantha was going to fly away, or at least her wrap would, and that she would run inside as the other guests began to do. The tablecloths peeled off the clips that held them to the tables, and the napkins jumped to the ground like scared frogs. Some of the glasses overturned and spilled the wine. Still, the musicians were reluctant to stop playing, reminiscent of the orchestra on the Titanic. When I asked her if she wanted to seek shelter under an awning, she rested her hand on mine and stroked it gently. "No way. I'm here to dance. Aren't you?"

We started dating almost immediately, seeing each other on weekends. I often visited her in Marseille, where she lived then, and other times she was the one hitting the road. More rarely, we met halfway. We went to Bruges, which we loved, and to Zurich during the worst cold spell in the last fifty years. It was easy to hang out with Samantha. She didn't care too much what we did as long as her coffee was ready when she got up. You didn't want to cross her in the morning.

I didn't work at Junot yet. I had this horrible sales position at an electrical equipment firm—me who can't replace a light bulb—but I was already becoming interested in wine and hoping that my *École de Commerce* diploma would take me a lot further. Where, I wasn't sure. In almost every photo from those days I'm wearing the orange backpack I'd bargained for in Marrakesh, as if I'm always ready to go. I didn't realize then that it was full of stones.

I spared Michele the more intimate details. I didn't tell her that day, or any other thereafter, that at home Samantha was much naughtier than I was. She often surprised me with sexy lingerie and erotic toys. At twenty-five, I didn't need much encouragement to cover all the bases. The rest of the time, we dreamed about our future. Would it be by the sea or in the mountains? House or condo? How many children did we want? I said three. One time she suggested four. Dreaming was so easy and fun.

After a year, she moved with me to Alsace and got a job restoring the choir stalls at Saint Etienne. I think those were our happiest days, in our studio on the canal. It was tiny and damp, actually terrible, but the lack of space became an advantage for us. It forced us to live glued to each other. It may sound crazy, but we enjoyed being crowded. We still needed to touch each other then.

"I'm very tactile too," Michele interrupted.

We got married in the Luberon, where Samantha was from, eleven months later. Talk about being crowded—the tiny church we chose couldn't fit everyone in who attended. Apparently, as we were told after the wedding, Samantha's aunt fainted during the ceremony due to the suffocating heat and had to be taken out to the cloister, the same one where we had the photo shoot later. Samantha wore a simple white strapless dress. Although I am not an expert on gowns or necklines, I do know that she shone on our wedding day.

As we left the church, we were greeted by a shower of rice and rose petals. The priest wasn't happy about the rice. Then came the tsunami of kisses and congratulations.

Samantha looked very happy surrounded by her friends and her two sisters, one of whom had come all the way from Toronto just for the wedding. Clearly, the groom is just a figurehead in the bride's show.

My mother pulled me by the arm. "You are married," she said proudly, as if it were her achievement, not mine.

Her comment surprised me. I thought she was going to feel a little sorry that her only son was leaving the nest.

"Congratulations, son," my father added. He kissed me, which is something he almost never did.

May they rest in peace. They both died way too early.

As I closed the door of our suite late that evening, I was fulfilled. I had married a beautiful woman—a doll really—and the first day of the rest of our lives started right then. We could now begin to make our dreams come true. Samantha lay naked on our bed, only her veil and her shoes still on. She threw a shoe up in the air. When the other one hit my forehead, she laughed. She blew me a sexy kiss, she parted her knees, and she spread her arms as wide as she could. "Come here, Love."

But I was exhausted and refused to dance.

Out of all my memories, I carefully selected for Michele just a few: the meeting at my cousin's wedding, the outline of the early months, the priest's reaction to the rice, and the romantic details of our cozy studio overlooking the canal. I gave her the fairy tale version, the sugar coated one everyone wants to hear.

"And why was it over?" she asked.

"It just ended," I said, shrugging. Then I changed the subject to my daughter Christine.

"You must be a great father," she said. She would repeat that many times over the following two years.

"You know what it feels like, right?"

She rolled down the window for a moment.

"You are very lucky to live here. It's a beautiful region. Look around. It's a shame you're alone."

"I have friends. There is life after divorce!" I hurried to say, faking a smile.

"Do you always act so animated?"

I was reluctant to admit that she was right, and I was, in fact, alone. How did she know? I didn't remember her asking that, only if I was married.

I told her about François and Bernadette in general terms, just to keep the conversation alive.

"We are the Three Musketeers," I said.

The truth is that François and Bernadette can't stand each other, so the three of us rarely get together. François says that Bernadette is a bitch named after a "bleached blonde prostitute." He probably has his reasons to feel that way, but in my opinion, Bernadette is rather the name of a saint, although an angel she's not. In turn, she says she can't stand "that ruminant," a reference to François' fondness for all sorts of herbs. He always carries in his car a hot water thermos and a metal case with an assortment of teas and medicinal plants. He has a remedy for every discomfort. Does your belly hurt? Ginger and cardamom. Low defenses, maybe? Infused rosemary. He's a good guy, François. He was very supportive during my divorce. He insists that I sign up for those dating apps.

"Not everyone is looking for sex," he says.

"Not everyone is looking for love," I reply.

Somehow, despite all of his advice, he keeps calling me on Fridays in case I feel like pizza or meeting at the Varadero for a mojito. He loves his mojitos! When he finishes one, he chews the leftover peppermint. The bottom line is that he is as alone as I am but, as he puts it, less droopy. When I argue that it's thanks to the carotenes in peppermint and sex has nothing to do with the shine of his skin, he gets angry. "Peppermint has no carotenes, you stupid ass, but it works great for flatulence and menstrual pain."

The best thing about François is that he knows who I am. I agree with him that Bernadette is not what you'd call easy. Not only does she tell you what to do, but she also drags you into it. If you share a fantasy with her, she'll conspire to make it come true. One of her mottos is, "Be careful what you wish for because Bernadette can make it happen." I find it annoying that she refers to herself in the third person, like a contemporary Nero, but her message is appealing. It must be that I am a coward, but not about everything. She would do anything for me and, for better or worse, she sometimes does. She would wink for me at a bar if she could and say that spicy word that I dare not. She would even have sex with someone in my place if that could make me feel alive again. She believes in me. "André, honey, who wouldn't like to sleep with you? I would."

It was actually Bernadette who ended up convincing me by FaceTime to make this trip to New York that I just returned from.

"What is the worst thing that can happen to you? Isn't your friend Lucy there? Stay with her! You need a change of scenery. You're stuck again."

"But I don't even know where Dawson lives," I objected.

"Can you just forget about Dawson and John, please! You don't know them. Think of yourself. And Michele. Although it's a bit weird ..."

I didn't need to ask for clarification.

"Why didn't she tell him herself?" she continued. "Especially if she knew where to find him and was about to kick the bucket."

"I can't believe she's passed away, Bernadette," I said with the sole intention of making it clear that ladies die; they don't kick buckets.

Bernadette went on insisting that something else was wrong, that it was illogical for Michele to ask me to go see John instead of Dawson because no matter how much she regretted giving John up for adoption, her "son, son"—she tapped the air with her index finger while she said that—was Dawson. "Any mother will tell you exactly what I just said." When I tell Bernadette tomorrow morning that she was right on, she'll get all cocky. I can already hear her say, "Didn't I tell you? Bernadette knew it all along."

"But in all this time you must have had your own Constance, I suppose," Michele asked when she noticed that I was going off on a tangent with all this musketeer stuff.

Why did she want to know? I hoped she wasn't one of those old ladies who get turned on by younger men.

"Some, not many."

I omitted the details. It was too early to disclose that after my divorce I had dated three ex-girlfriends and had slept with two of them. With the third one I'd also tried, but I couldn't get it up. I guess at that point I already cared whether I was fed apples or oranges. Antoinette had caused, in the good old days, the earth to move. We had lived through some memorable afternoons at her parents' apartment on rue Gambetta, so it wasn't just that sequels are never any good, it's that I killed those precious memories of my youth altogether at the stroke of a pen—or lack thereof, in this case. We can never take things for granted, can we?

Michele volunteered that she was a widow. Hadn't I already witnessed that scene in some movie? That was the part when the Merry Widow makes a pass at the leading man.

"Could we stop for a while?" she said suddenly. "The landscape is so beautiful that I don't want to just watch it go by."

"Here?"

There was no room on the shoulder for us to stop. I had the feeling that she wanted to talk to me without Armand listening.

"I'd like to be part of it, even if it's only for a couple of minutes," she added, her eyes bright with excitement. "Would it be possible?" She rested her cheek on the glass and looked out the window pensively.

A ditch separated the road from the vineyards. I tapped Armand on his back twice. It was hard as a rock. I pointed at the dusty detour which started just a few yards ahead, past a ruined house of which only the burnt wooden beams and three of the outer walls remained. Then the path wandered the vineyards forming an immense meander and finally merging with the horizon. The Mercedes S skidded to the right onto the stony path, lifting a cloud of dust. The ground was unusually dry, as if the rain of the previous week had dodged that corner. After about a quarter of a mile, we took a second detour. Shortly after, we stopped in a small clearing. In summer, the country looked like a beautiful garden. Michele was agitated. She emptied her bag over the seat. Armand watched the scene through the rearview mirror.

"Looking for your phone, Madame?" he asked in his heavily accented Provençal English. He was holding the iPhone Michele had given him to charge. Michele sighed in relief. She grabbed her phone and stuffed everything back into her tiny Prada pocketbook: lipstick, eyeshadow, tissues, a hand sanitizer, some Advil, and a Ziplock bag with a dozen marble-like pills. Amazingly, everything fit. I realized then that a photo had fallen on the floor of the car. It stood out against the car's dark upholstery. I reached down to pick it up. It was one of those old Polaroid snapshots.

"Who is he?" I asked and handed her the photo of the boy on the bicycle. She ripped it out of my hands and hurriedly put it back in her bag.

"He's very handsome," I said to soften her reaction. "Is he your son?"

"This was a zillion years ago," she replied and grabbed her cell phone and her hat with the big blue tie. "I don't even know why I carry it on me."

Armand passed by my window and turned around the vehicle to open Michele's door. It was so windy that he was squinting, his tie was blowing away, and his shirt clung tightly to his torso.

"What's his name?" I asked increasingly curious.

"Oh My God, it's so windy!" she said when Armand opened her door. A gust of wind whipped into the car and cooled the interior off. Michele held Armand's hand and started to get out. When I thought I'd be left without an answer, she turned her face to me and said:

"How do you like Dawson? But feel free to call him what you please."

The coldness of her answer made me think they weren't getting along, so I decided to change the subject.

"Watch out for your hat. It could end up in Germany," I warned her, and I got ready to become one more brushstroke in the improvised country landscape that Michele had painted in her imagination.

It was windier than I'd thought, but unlike the stormy air on the day I'd met Samantha, the wind blew steadily this time.

"Look at the sky. Not even Constable's can top this!" she exclaimed and began to walk towards the shelter of the vines. She walked briskly, quite ahead of me. With one hand she kept the hat on her head, and with the other she tried to keep the wind from lifting her skirt. The wind drew the fabric against her legs and her pretty butt. "She must have been a beautiful woman," I thought. She still was. Suddenly, the vines stirred, and the hat popped off her head, but Michele caught it in the air, looking amused.

"This is nothing compared to when it's windy at home," she said when I reached her. "I must show you San Francisco."

"They say it's very pretty," I said not very cleverly. It was amazing that Michele saw a future in our Picard-induced meeting.

"Look around. Oh, oh, oh," she said as if she were beginning to reach orgasm. "I love the countryside. Did you know that I was raised on a farm in North Dakota?"

I had a hard time imagining Michele in a rural environment. I couldn't picture her as a young girl surrounded by pigs and manure, dressed in jeans, plaid shirt, and muddy shoes, a little like Dorothy in the Wizard of Oz. In my mind, her animals turned a bubblegum pink color, smooth and clean, more like jelly beans.

"We had horses," she added and killed my sugary pigs with those three words. What would she have looked like at eighteen, or possibly twenty, naked on horseback?

"Do you ride?" she asked, and by means of that simple question she got me on her horse. I think I never got off.

"Sometimes. Not much, really. You?"

"Not anymore," she said, "but I loved it." She closed her eyes to smell a grape leaf, then let go of the vine with its juicy bunches of Gewürztraminer.

"It just scares me," I admitted.

"Does it, really?" She smiled in a somewhat mocking way.

"Once one got out of control, and I almost fell off."

"It probably was a young horse."

"I just know it was called Portento: shiny black, tall, with thick, long hind legs. Gorgeous! But as soon as I rode it, I knew I was going to regret it. It wasn't exactly docile. It shook its neck violently and lifted its legs several feet off the ground. Since that time, I haven't tried to ride again."

"Was it male or female?"

"Does it matter?" I asked.

"Honey, you're so funny. Of course, it matters." I hadn't meant to be funny. "You didn't make it clear who was in charge, that's all. Next time, show your authority. Authority and love, that's the secret."

She started walking again. Now we were walking side by side along the furrow between the vines. Michele set the pace.

"May I offer you another tip?" she said. "If what you fancy is a quiet walk, next time ride an older horse."

What was she suggesting? I cleared my throat, but I didn't have the chance to ask her.

"It was the perfect stop," she said abruptly. "Now, if you'd like, please take me to Fort Schoenenbourg."

We returned to the car and resumed our journey. Michele changed after that break. She stopped digging in my personal life and inquiring about Samantha, Christine, and my poor love life, and she opened up. And how! From then and until we arrived at the fort, she told me some episodes of her life that I'd only share with my closest friends, but even then she managed to keep her distance and continued to play that strange dissonance between discourse and manners which drove me crazy. Some of the stories were on the verge of being so explicitly private that even Bernadette herself would blush, like her affair on a beach in San Diego with two brothers, whom she called Castor and Pollux.

"Funny names," I said.

"Their real names were Matt and Jason O'Brian."

"Ok …" I said puzzled.

"They were twins, but only one made me feel immortal. I assure you that Jason was the son of Zeus. Divine Pollux."

I, who knew nothing about Greek mythology, tried to understand why she trusted me with all that. Didn't she have anyone else to talk about sex with? Armand looked at me in the rearview mirror halfway between amazed and amused. I smiled back at him. That's exactly how I felt. Was this chance meeting a bad joke or an opportunity? Maybe someone up there was getting a lot of fun from watching the two of us interact inside the car. Michele and I had nothing in common. She was the epitome of a liberated woman, while I ... let's just talk about something else.

When Armand finally stopped the car in the small parking lot circled by trees, I felt relieved. This didn't seem like a very popular place. There were no more than five or six cars and a motorhome. A sign announced where we were: "Fort Schoenenbourg. Maginot Line."

"Sometimes you don't know your own country," I admitted at the fort's entrance. I had never been there before.

"There is always a first time for everything," Michele said. "Don't be ashamed. Have you noticed that the wind is no longer blowing? Not here."

It wasn't shame what I was experiencing. It was rather a vague and unpleasant sense of ignorance.

"Should we enter?" she asked. "You'll see what an impressive work this is. A true paradigm of pointless resistance to the inevitable and of the obstinacy of the human being."

I looked in my pocket for a twenty euro bill to buy the tickets. Picard had told me not to let her pay for anything. Why did the rich always get everything for free?

When I was about to pay the admission fee, Michele changed her mind:

"Wait," she said. "Let's sit for a moment before we go in."

There was no bench to sit on, but Michele turned out to be less fussy than I thought. We sat on the floor to the left of the door. We rested our backs against the cement of the bunker. The guard gave us a disapproving look but didn't say anything. Michele complained that her shoes were killing her and took them off. She hadn't walked all that much, so I don't know how they could hurt. She had small feet and impeccable nails. She pulled her skirt up, just above her knees. She looked at me. I looked at her. Then she stared up at the growing clouds, and I kept busy following an ant that lifted a leaf several times its own size. This alternation of silence and soliloquy made me a little uncomfortable. She finally spoke:

"I wanted to come here for my father. He served in Europe with the 8th Infantry division during World War II. He was severely injured in the leg, like Saint Ignatius, and like Ignatius, he lived to tell the tale. I am trying to understand why he was the way he was."

I started to open my mouth. She anticipated my question.

"Hard. Protective. Committed. Stern. In my travels, I visit places with a warlike past: Normandy, Auschwitz, Terezin ..."

"Poor Jews," I said.

"Also the gypsies. And the homosexuals. About ten thousand homosexuals were sent to the concentration camps. They were marked with a pink triangle and were the lowest caste. Can you imagine something like that? It happened not so long ago."

"Horrible," I replied with unblinking eyes and resisting the urge to scratch.

Michele noticed that I was a little tense.

"Are you Jewish?"

"Why?"

"I don't know. Your nose?"

"My nasal septum is slightly crooked," I said and covered it with my hand. Michele gently pushed my hand away.

"I find your nose beautiful."

I got in profile, giving her my best angle.

"The Maginot Line was a resounding failure," she summed up, and began to put her shoes back on.

"All these fortifications must have been of some use."

She sighed. I think she found me naive.

"They were absolutely useless. All these bunkers, tunnels and trenches along hundreds of miles were a futile effort. The Germans invaded your beautiful country through the back door. Some outcomes simply cannot be avoided because they are in the nature of things. Do you know what I'm talking about?"

Yes, I did. Of course I knew.

"Things can be changed," I said, "and I can't see what's natural in the invasion of some barbarians."

She looked at me softly, like a mother at the rebellious comment of her child.

"We can build dikes and barriers, but water will continue to flood the streets of Venice during the *acqua alta.* And the only thing we can do when that happens is to put on rubber boots in order not to get our feet wet."

"Or not go to Venice," I said, and I was left with the feeling that talking with Michele was like traveling the world in the course of a few minutes.

"But that's very sad," she said. "May I ask you something, André?"

"I suppose," I replied as I stood up. Michele held out her hand so that I could help her get up. She took off and put back on her loose shoe. Then she pulled her phone out of her purse.

"Stand right there," she said, pointing at the bunker. "I'll take your picture." She took a couple of steps back. "Smile," she added, hiding behind her cell phone. And while I showed her my teeth, she asked me, "André, honey, what is your Maginot Line?"

It was around 2:00 pm when our visit to the fort was over. It was getting late for lunch. Armand suggested his brother-in-law's bistro in Hohwiller. The restaurant was a little house made of stone and wood located right in the center of town. In the two tables which were still occupied, the guests were already sipping their coffee. On the right-hand side of the dining room was a smoke-blackened chimney. At the far end, a large window overlooked a courtyard with a large fig tree whose leaves were crushed against the glass. One could almost feel the pain of the tree and that of the glass. The restaurant smelled of duck—the house specialty—and of moss, don't ask me why. It was cozy, but at first, I wasn't sure Michele would like it. I only knew she was pleased with the choice of restaurants because she rested her arms on the table in a big, open circle when we sat by the window.

"Very cute," she said. "It has that French charm. Like you."

Armand introduced us to the chef. He came forward with his chef's hat on to welcome us. He looked both delighted and nervous. He could not have made a career as a public speaker, that was clear. Michele interrupted him with a smile.

"We are dying to try your cooking," she said, and got up to go to the bathroom.

The chef said goodbye to Armand and offered to feed him at the bar.

"Special, huh?" Armand whispered before leaving. I smiled. "I don't know what you give her, but she seems delighted with you. In the two days I've been driving her around, she has barely spoken to me."

I shrugged.

"I'm sure she appreciates your good driving."

The last guests got up a few minutes after Michele returned from the ladies' room. We were left with the whole dining room to ourselves.

We ordered a salad and duck breast. And champagne. Michele insisted on the champagne.

"With the duck?" I asked.

"As long as the duck doesn't mind," she replied jokingly.

Personally, I would have paired the duck breast with a syrah or with a pinot noir from Bourgogne, even with a Riesling if I'd been compelled to choose a white. I opted for a Gasset Brut Excellence to make Michele happy. It was the most basic champagne in its range, but by far the best choice on the restaurant's reduced wine list, which only had four sparkling wines, two of them so basic that I questioned the quality of the cooking itself. The Gasset seemed right for that casual lunch. The complexity of the bird required a fresh yet necessarily robust counterpoint.

The only waiter in the restaurant soon brought it. I felt the bottle. It was at optimum temperature. Thank goodness. I uncorked it myself and served it. Michele watched in silence, apparently pleased by my expertise in handling the bottle.

"I was watching your hands," she said when her glass was full.

I waited for the second part of the comment, but it never came. I picked up my champagne glass and saw my reflection in the round base of the glass. My eyes were distorted and droopy—an optical effect like those of magic mirrors in old amusement parks.

"If there's something I absolutely love, it is the hands of a man," she said. She took a quick sip and fanned her face with her hand. "Let's talk about something else," she added with fake embarrassment.

But Michele didn't want to talk about anything else. She wanted to talk about sex. With me. Before lunch.

"I can't believe it's been two years since I've been alone with a man," Michele said as casually as she would have said that a fig tree produces figs.

I was absorbed in my reflection when she said that, still trapped inside the glass circle. That's exactly how I felt those days: stuck and lacking air. The bubbles rose to the surface of the champagne as quickly as oxygen fled away from my lungs.

I hadn't been with anyone for a long time either, but I didn't tell her that.

I looked up only to find Michele's incisive eyes gazing at me.

"Since your husband died?" I asked.

"Since Ted died. Didn't I tell you about Ted?"

I shook my head. She had quite a collection of lovers.

"I'm something like a black widow. She looked at me through her champagne. If I were you, I'd be careful."

"Then I am glad that we don't have that kind of relationship."

I surprised myself with my choice of the word "relationship." At most, this was a business lunch, some sort of deference to the specialized press. It would never have taken place if Michele's brother wasn't the director of such an important magazine.

"Ted was innately talented. He knew what keys to press to play the right music."

It was ironic that fate had seated me in front of such a sexual person, but I couldn't blame her. What did she know about my absurd self-imposed celibacy?

"Well, good for you, right?" I said with a mischievous smile. "Virtuosity doesn't abound."

Speaking so lightly of someone who was dead felt somewhat wrong. Michele talked about Ted warmly, as she later would about other lovers. She always emphasized the positive. In Ted's case, I noticed that this affection didn't turn into love simply because of the lack of time, just like grape juice needs to ferment in order to become wine.

"It's hard to see your loved ones die. It's like losing your fingertips. I have been advised to start seeking out younger people. What about you?" she asked.

"What about me?"

I hesitated between directing our conversation to more conventional topics or playing along. Deep down, Michele's unusual ways amused me.

"You don't like talking about yourself, do you?"

"I don't have much to say," I said, "but I love listening to you. What a life!"

"I guess in my youth I was a rebel, yes. My God, André, that was centuries ago. The pill gave us freedom to be like you, and just get pleasure without risking the consequences. And men—she stopped talking and smiled knowingly—men loved it, at a time when many women still used sex, or the promise of sex, as their passport to the altar."

Her eyes lit up. What could she be remembering? "And then there was you," I said.

"And then there was me, yes. The crazy, intrepid Michele. But I was young at the time. Then I got married and ..."

"And the rest is history."

"I was very determined to make it work."

"And it did, didn't it?"

"Sex and economic issues are the two main causes of divorce in the U.S." I was taken aback by her academic response. "Richard and I never lacked one or the other. In thirty-one years of marriage."

"And what about love? Where does it fit?"

"Love is wonderful. I hope you find it one day. I've been lucky enough to fall in love twice."

I felt a pang of envy. It was similar to that of hunger. "It's hard to keep the flame of love alive for so many years," I said.

"Who said I was in love with Richard? But I loved him. And as I told you, I was determined to make my marriage work even though nobody bet on the success of our relationship. Maybe that's why I tried harder."

She had some more champagne. She was pensive.

"Time goes by extremely fast, André. When I look back at my life, I rarely regret what I have done—and I have done some wild things, believe me—but rather what I did not do: the unspoken word, the kiss not given, the chance I did not take."

I took a sip. It tasted bitter, although it wasn't.

"I was bubbly like champagne," she said, tilting the glass, dipping her gaze in the drink as if searching for her past. "I have gradually lost some of my bubbles."

"Thank God," I thought. Gently, I took her glass from her hands. At first she resisted, but then she opened her fist and let it go.

"Do you want to see something?" I asked.

I poured the champagne into an empty wine glass that shouldn't have been on the table. The bubbles disappeared instantly.

"Now it looks like white wine," I said and winked at her. "See? I can take your bubbles away at will."

"André the magician," she said. She pretended to wave a magic wand in the air.

I put the champagne back into the fluted glass. It bubbled again. Michele clasped her hands in a hint of applause and sighed in relief.

"They need an imperfection to hold on to," I said.

She looked at me as if she hadn't quite understood.

"The bubbles, I mean. That's why the bottoms of all champagne glasses are scraped on purpose. Can you see? They are not perfect."

"As my father said, 'Never trust people who seem perfect, because they surely have something to hide.' That's why I have always run away from people who put on a nice mask. Until now."

"I just showed you that the container is as important as the content."

"Are we still talking about champagne?" she asked as the waiter left the salads in front of us.

"Seriously, thank you for returning the bubbles to me," she added flirtatiously. "Now I am in debt to you, and I'll have to think how to settle it."

After the salad and the duck, it was time for dessert. Time had truly flown.

"May I have a little dish with five cherries?" she asked the waiter.

"How come so few?" I asked.

"I love cherries. They are my favorite fruit in the universe, but if I eat more than five, they don't agree with me. More than five and my stomach gets terribly upset."

"You know what they say, 'too much of a good thing ...'"

After lunch, we dropped her at her hotel.

"I've had a great day," I told her at the door.

"I am glad because you are not going to get rid of me any time soon."

She said it as a joke, or that's how I initially took it, but when she reached her hand out to say goodbye, she added:

"Would you like to come with me to Argentina?"

Michele, like the bubbles in champagne, needed an imperfection to hold onto. I had a few, luckily for me not too obvious to the poorly trained eye. Michele quickly learned how to use them to her advantage and gradually slipped into my life. In her defense, I made room for her too. A few days after our first meeting, she sent me an email. Then another. And then yet one more until we corresponded daily. In each one, she managed to convey the same message: how important I was to her. At first I didn't take her too seriously, but she kept repeating it until it soaked in. Within a few weeks, I was totally convinced that I had become a key in her life, and I started to give her back a tiny part of the affection she poured on me. That's why I began to love her—to pay her back, just like you'd pay an overdue loan.

One day, she repeated the offer she'd made at her hotel's door after our trip to Fort Schoenenbourg. She chose the right time. It was Saturday night, and I felt helpless. Sometimes, almost always in the evening and out of pure loneliness, the little man who has lived in my stomach since who knows when wakes up and screams. It's a silent scream like in Munch's picture, almost a cry. Whenever I feel that way, I—the big man who neither shouts nor cries—do nothing except wait. I just wait, with a glass of wine handy, often for hours, for the little man to get tired and finally fall asleep.

Argentina. The name itself carried an echo of noble metal and opportunity. The trip looked so wonderful that anyone would have found it difficult to refuse, plus I could combine it with my Christmas holidays and still return in time to spend New Year's with Christine. She made her invitation even easier for me to accept. She said she needed a translator. I happened to speak Spanish because my maternal grandparents were from Spain. She added that my wine knowledge would be helpful as well, and that it was always wiser for someone of her sex and age to travel in the company of a man.

"I will take care of everything else. Don't worry about anything."

To not worry about anything. That did it. The trip—Michele herself when I think of it—was an escape route. It was, as I see it now, a flight to nowhere, a ticket to leave Venice during the *acqua alta*, to use one of her favorite travel similes.

I made it clear that I could only offer her my friendship. She laughed.

"Don't be ridiculous. What else do you think I want?"

"To get into your bed, do you have any doubt?" Bernadette warned me when I told her.

"If you don't go, I will. The trip sounds amazing," said François, when his turn came to express his opinion.

Who in their right mind believed there could be sex? I was forty years old. She was sixty-four and would turn sixty-five right after South America.

"My little André," Bernadette sighed, "sometimes you're so cute."

Three months later, Michele and I met in Argentina. I rode the TGV from Strasbourg to Paris, flew over the Atlantic to Buenos Aires, and boarded the plane to Mendoza at the last minute. I soon started to feel like a tree pulled up from its roomy terracotta pot and transplanted into a tiny flowerpot, the roots crowded into a handful of soil. Michele's world was totally different from mine. It wasn't just the age difference—after all, it's the age of the spirit what counts—or the class distinction. Her pockets were deeper, but I was just as educated. It was rather a matter of feeling comfortable in your own skin. Michele possessed the bearing of a golden eagle. She filled the room with her presence and, when she spoke, it was as if she spread her wings, and there was no room for anyone else, except for maybe some simpleton like me whom she had decided to shelter within her feathers. Michele was more read, more traveled, had "loved" well and often, and had been loved too. By her side, I sometimes felt out of place, properly dressed for each occasion, but always under the impression that no matter what tie I chose to wear, she would be the one to knot it. When she learned that I had arrived at the hotel, she stood at the door of my room, looked at me from head to foot, and stretched out her arms as much as possible. I hugged her. Wasn't that what she expected? Surprisingly, I felt comfortable wrapped in the blue warmth that she gave off. She didn't brush me off. Quite the opposite. She stroked my back, whispered, "I know," and I felt comforted, like a child who had previously been lost in a department store.

In Mendoza, the days drifted by between visits of wineries, lunches with cloth napkins, and starched sheets. There were leisurely breakfasts at the vineyards served in porcelain tea sets with an English hallmark. The hours meandered, as there was no hurry, and soon I got used to that lazy pace. There was no pain, and to be honest no excessive joy either, but I found the anesthesia pleasantly safe. I didn't want to suffer, even at the expense of not pursuing happiness. Michele, as promised, took care of everything. Inside her protective bubble I avoided, and sometimes almost forgot, that one day I'd have to deal with my paralyzing fears. One day.

We didn't do too many things. We talked. We ate. We drank. Between food and drink, I tried to make her laugh. And many times, I did. I loved to see her eyes squint and her shoulders lift. She laughed with restraint, with her chest rather than with her mouth, as if she were holding back a cough or was afraid of losing her bearing if she showed too many teeth. When I wanted her to laugh openly, I gave her a little bit of my sweet talk and then, briefly, the arch of her lips unglued, and her eyes lit up. I took advantage of that fleeting moment in which she seemed happy and carefree, and her guard was down to try to discern what moved her inside.

Michele trotted out her favorite subject too soon, sometimes even before my first coffee. The first morning she announced with great fanfare that she had decided to retire from the "bedroom pleasures." She liked to say things with ceremony. I wasn't surprised she'd used the word "retire." Sex had been so important to her for such a long time that it was only logical she referred to it as a career more than as a hobby.

"It's no longer worth the work it requires," she said as she spread apricot jam on an English muffin.

"A withdrawal in time ..."

She didn't hesitate.

"I was very good at it, you know?" she said and took a bite of her muffin in slow motion, or so it seemed to me.

Each one of my attempts to discuss other matters, especially Dawson, fell on deaf ears. The most recent events have shed new light on her reasons to be so discreet, but back then I didn't understand her ice-cold relationship with her son. My interest in knowing more about him was always met with a blank gaze. I told her things about Christine to try to connect with her maternal instinct, but it was useless. She always ended up talking about love and sex, and I listened to her. Maybe that was my mistake. I always listened to her. The harder I tried to talk about Dawson, the more she wanted to know why I had no known partner or the slightest desire to find one.

"And what about sex? You're too young to live a sexless life, André, dear."

I imagine that Michele wanted to solve that anomaly and planned a dinner for three with a friend of hers, coincidentally also divorced, on our last evening in Mendoza. "We saw each other for the last time at the Stop AIDS gala. You'll see; she's lovely," she'd told me in the morning when she'd announced our commitment to attend. "And very attractive."

Dinner was in the restaurant at the golf club. We had decided to meet there because Michele had a cocktail party at the same place right before.

"Your mother is already waiting for you," the maitre d' said when I arrived.

Carol came a minute later, squeezed in a tight flesh-colored dress with Swarovski crystals around the neckline. The fabric's tone barely contrasted with the paleness of her skin. You couldn't tell the dress from the woman. All in all, a poor choice.

"You look divine," Michele said, "Carolina Herrera?"

Carol smiled. "What a joy to see you, Michele. It really is a small world."

"I am wearing an André Broussard," said Michele. She raised her arms, looked up at the ceiling, and remained still like the statue of a goddess for two seconds. Then she laughed and introduced us.

Carol immediately struck me as a woman who doubted herself. I knew it because she looked at me with a mix of excitement and distrust when we were introduced. She liked me, but something about me didn't fit. "I don't know what makes you think every woman falls for you," Samantha would tell me if she were with me. I thought that Carol had probably had a terrible track record with men. If she was unable to pick a dress that suited her well, how could she succeed in finding a life partner? I mean, the dress was beautiful, just not for her. I analyzed her features in more detail. As a matter of fact, she wasn't ugly at all. She was about my age and had some class but not nearly as much as Michele. She lacked pedigree. Michele, in a simple black silk blouse, more than beat her in elegance. I gave her face a B minus and her body a B plus, and I was immediately glad that a machine that read my thoughts had not yet been invented. She spoke very spiritedly, constantly waving her hands. A small platinum cross rested on her cleavage. Would she take it off before having sex?

"So the two of you ..." Carol asked after the presentations.

"I'm saving the seat for the right woman," Michele answered.

It bothered me to no end that Michele gave herself a role that I hadn't asked her to play. She liked to play ambiguity in front of other people. There was nothing between us.

"It seems that he's taking his time," she added sarcastically.

"I am sure you have many girls lining up outside your door," said Carol.

"What makes you think so?" I asked.

The waiter handed Michele a black napkin and Carol a white one.

"I love these details," Michele said, and briefly explained that the reason was she was wearing black.

"Now you'll tell me that you are very demanding," Carol said.

The conversation was heading just where I didn't want it to go.

"Not especially," I said.

I thought that by giving such vague answers, they'd get that I didn't want to discuss my relationship status.

"And then?" Carol said.

"And you?" I rushed to ask. "How did you meet?"

They both looked at each other and smiled mischievously, but they didn't say a word.

"I still have hope," Carol said with a flash of disenchantment in her eyes. "What do you think, André, is there hope for us?" she asked in a teenage voice. Why had she suddenly changed the tone of her voice? Could she be one of those women who in bed intermingle gasps with short words and speak like a breathless prostitute, as if she manned the phone on a sex hotline? I hated that kind of women.

I was not going to give them the satisfaction of saying yes. I weighed answering something like "where there's life there's hope," but I decided to shut up and try to change the subject.

"Can I tell you a joke?" I asked.

"We're talking about seduction now," Michele said sharply.

She caught me off guard. Carol noticed my puzzlement and looked at me sweetly. I smiled back at her, grateful. She was tapping her cross. I pushed the bangs off my forehead and loosened the knot of my tie. She flipped her crucifix. I inadvertently separated my knees. Michele returned the smile that I had given Carol, as if we were, the three of us, apexes of the same triangle and were united by some kind of universal love. I couldn't help but think for a moment of her threesome with Castor and Pollux.

"I'm the least flirtatious person in the world," I said, "so I'm afraid I don't have much to add to the topic of seduction." I tightened my tie again. I struggled to smile warmly, but Michele gave me a questioning look. This time I wasn't going to get away with just a charming smile. That night she expected answers.

"Have you been divorced a long time?" Carol asked me.

"Two years," Michele answered for me.

"White or red?" I asked, resorting to the wine list.

"Do you mind if I ask you why?" Carol insisted.

"We should have a malbec," I said.

"Your friend is a specialist in passing the buck."

"He's lucky he's funny telling jokes," Michele said, stroking my arm. "It's too bad I already know them all."

"It was an amicable divorce," I replied so as not to seem too rude.

"Come on, sweetheart," Michele said, "Carol asked you why, not how."

Why, why, why. Well, because I couldn't take it anymore—I wanted to tell them—and succumbed to a night of sturdy hands. It was one of those rare nights of super moon, avid, fat, and treacherous moon. Under the moonlight, I heard, "Do not fear," and I stopped shaking and opened myself to the joy of that other, so long-awaited love.

"We stopped loving each other," I said, and put an end to that part of the conversation. I swallowed. It tasted like salt and spearmint.

I managed to take control of the rest of the evening, and from that moment on, things went smoothly. After all, I was quite good at entertaining. It was no surprise that Picard always chose me whenever we had to keep a customer happily busy. I carried the conversation with the ladies and made sure the glasses wouldn't empty. I even managed to have some fun along the way. We discussed my work in the cellar and Carol's as an interior designer. She'd come from Houston to decorate a tasting room. We talked about France and America, about this and that—but not too much of this nor an excess of that—and even fixed the world a little, but just enough. At our age we had already accepted it, meanness and all. And yes, I came up with a couple of jokes that Michele didn't know.

"I can't recall the last time I laughed this hard," Carol said red faced and satisfied. "Let's toast. Here's to love!"

"And to sex, for those of you who are still active," Michele added, joining her glass to her friend's.

I felt the pressure of adding something ingenious and original to the toast. Since I couldn't think of anything, I decided to seize the moment to make something clear.

I raised my glass. I looked at Michele and then at Carol. Their pupils shone in anticipation.

"Ladies, here's to friendship."

My toast didn't raise the bet and fell on them like a jar of cold water. I could tell by the lack of enthusiasm when our glasses clinked and by the awkward silence that followed. In the meantime, I kept myself busy admiring the fineness of the dishes' edges and the careful arrangement of the red plaid-ribboned centerpiece.

"I'm going to the ladies' room," said Carol. "Are you coming with me?"

She softly rested her hand on my forearm and left it there for a few seconds. Was she talking to me? My pulse accelerated.

"Do you mind if we leave you alone for a little while?" Michele asked.

Why would I care? Loneliness was my natural state.

"Not at all," I said. "You need two people in the confessional."

Michele and Carol walked away to the bathroom, swinging their hips, navigating the other guests who, unlike me, did seem to have a purpose to be there. At the nearest table, a couple of lovebirds shared their saliva and a *crème brûlée*. Under the crystal chandelier, an old couple, surely on vacation, looked at each other over their reading glasses and tried to find in the dessert menu an excuse to say something. At the round table next to the window, two couples of friends laughed loudly. They must have been celebrating a birthday because the bald man blew out the candles on a cake—forty-five. I ran my fingers through my bangs, glad to have kept my hair.

What the hell was I doing there? I was tired of wasting my time. I wanted to leave, but it wasn't going to be easy.

Michele and Carol seemed very spirited when they returned to the table. They exchanged complicit glances, as if they'd just shared a big secret, and displayed that silly security of someone who is no longer a virgin. They were laughing.

"We know what's wrong with you," Michele announced.

"And we have the solution," Carol added.

"Now it's my turn to go to the bathroom, so if you'll excuse me …"

I made sure to overlap my comment with Carol's to create some confusion. I stood up. I pushed the chair away. I left my napkin on the table. When I was passing behind Michele's back and was already beginning to savor freedom, I noticed a strong pull on my hand. I felt the roughness of Michele's skin, the touch of her wedding ring, the rugged tablecloth on my knuckles, and her pretentious voice, rising above the murmur of the dining room.

"Samantha had to hurt you a great deal for you to run away from women the way you do."

When we finished dinner and Carol left, I was ready to call it a day but was dragged to the bar for a drink. The bar was a green velvet-lined room with mahogany tables and elegant waiters in double breasted jackets and bow ties.

"What do you think about Carol?"

"She's great."

I flipped through the cocktail menu. It was longer than the Bible.

"She was very impressed with you. She found you very charming."

"Should I get something rum based or something whiskey-ish? What are you going to have?"

"She asked me if you were gay."

I took some peanuts from the bowl.

"I said you weren't," she added. "At least not that I knew."

I counted the peanuts in my hand. There were five. Three with skin and two skinless. I ate the two skinless ones.

"According to her, men like you are either gay or impotent," Michele continued.

I rested the three whole peanuts on top of a paper napkin. I peeled one and put it in my mouth. I chewed it. The pieces of this new peanut amalgamated with the two previous ones, and the resulting paste got stuck between my teeth.

"I think I'll have a Bloody Mary," she said.

"Bloody Mary and mojito, then," I said.

"I don't know about being impotent. I think you are not gay."

"These peanuts are a bit stale."

"Did you have fun tonight?"

"Oh, yes, very much so."

"She also wondered what would have happened if I were twenty years younger."

"And what did you say?"

"I told her that nothing would have happened. You would never have accepted my invitation."

"Should we order? My mouth is dry."

The next morning, I woke up early to catch our flight to Buenos Aires. We wanted to spend the last night of our stay in Argentina in the capital. I attributed my slight hangover to having mixed wine and mojitos, but perhaps it was simply lack of sleep.

I packed carelessly. I threw the tie in the bag with the dirty clothes and then stirred tie, socks, and underwear to impregnate the tie with the most pestilent smells of the human body. I hate to wear a tie on vacation, and since I can't always find the courage to act out of personal convictions, this was my way to make sure that I didn't wear one again. While packing my shirts, I remembered Carol: her dress clinging to charms that didn't interest me, her dancing hands, her carmine stained teeth. I felt the aftertaste of stale peanuts again. I closed the bag's zipper. I would leave those memories out. There were many Carols in the world, and none fit in my luggage. I picked up the suitcase from the bed and placed it next to the bedroom door. I hadn't bought anything, and yet it seemed heavier than at the beginning of the trip.

"You have been a great translator," Michele told me on the plane. She delivered her compliment with a wide smile. If you ask me, I hadn't been all that helpful. In the circles she frequented, English was widely, almost exclusively, used. I told her it had been easy and accepted the orange juice offered by the flight attendant. I was about to take the champagne, but I thought it was too early to drink alcohol even in our first-class microcosm. I stretched my legs and put my feet on the footrest, flipped through the plane's magazine, and opened the toiletries bag. It was packed with items that I wasn't going to use: a body lotion, an eye contour cream, a lip repair, socks, a sleeping mask, earplugs, a toothbrush kit that included a small mouthwash, a pen, and a notebook. Where was the limit between abundance and excess? I wished there were a similar set for the needs of the soul. I looked at Michele. She tilted her head and smiled warmly at me.

Soon, the plane began to gain speed on the runway. Behind the asphalted lane, the plain and dry fields started to move along the airplane's side, as if the plane and the landscape were racing against each other. I closed my eyes as the plane rose from the ground. I gave in to the slight dizziness roused by vertigo and adrenaline. It was a pleasant feeling that I wished I could replicate in my everyday life. Take off; fly; live. The noise of the wheels retracting brought me back to reality. I looked out the window. The city lights were still on. You could see water tanks and solar panels spread over the cracked soil, and toy sized cars on endless highways. Further out, the mountains looked like a huge, scary crocodile. As we gained altitude, Mendoza became tinier and tinier, and the curve of the planet appeared on the horizon. From these heights everything seemed more orderly, and you couldn't get a glimpse of the suffering of the people. The world looked beautiful.

"There's no reason we can't see it together," said the fortune teller sitting next to me, guessing my thoughts.

I didn't answer her immediately but, once again, I couldn't help thinking that Michele wanted too much, too soon. We hadn't completed this trip yet, and she had already planted the seed for the next one. And she had done it big time. Unlike me, she did know how to raise the bet.

I thanked her.

"Whenever you want," she said. "Remember that I will always be on your side."

For the moment, the world would have to wait. And Michele too. My heart was already in France. In three days, I'd have Picard stuck to my neck again. The contacts we'd made at the Vinexpo in Bordeaux and at the London Wine Fair in the Spring were beginning to bear fruit. If things went as planned, I'd soon be asking him for a promotion, not just a pay raise but also a change in my stupid job title. I tried not to think about my overflowing email inbox or my apartment. With so many thieves and squatters, I never went on a trip with peace of mind. But most of all, I wanted to see Christine after spending those days so far from her. Her Christmas break was almost over, and she'd soon be starting school again. She had not yet turned twelve, and puberty was already kicking in. Sometimes, she wore a push-up bra for her chestnut-sized breasts. To raise what, I didn't know, but I suppose at her age going from chickpeas to chestnuts was a huge step up. She'd given herself some blue highlights in her hair too. I wish I had dared to do something ballsy like that when I was a teenager, but my father would have told me to tone it down. I tried to be careful with my comments to Christine. Some stick and change your character forever.

I wrapped myself in the blanket. We were above the clouds now. I decided to ignore Michele for a while. Thinking about Christine was much more rewarding. She was a strange combination. She had a slightly deviated nasal septum—like me—and my honey-colored eyes and brown hair—well, brown and blue those days—but she was calm and sweet like Samantha and just as moody in the morning. Two more days and I'd be with her.

That relaxing time on the plane was precious because when we arrived in Buenos Aires, we immediately transferred to the hotel for check-in and lunch. Michele was quieter than usual. Or maybe it was me. Mentally, I was no longer there. After lunch, I was able to scrape a couple of hours of solitude and walk around the Palermo neighborhood. I liked having time for myself to do some people watching. The *porteños* were intense and contradictory. The driver who had picked us up at the airport, originally from Rosario, had defined them as Italians who speak Spanish and believe they live in Paris. I found his description most accurate. I regretted not having more time to ease into some street talk with my heavily accented Spanish, but Michele was waiting for me at 7:30 for dinner, so I rushed through the streets to be back at the hotel by 7:00. A box and a card rested on my bed. "Blue looks good on you," said the note signed by Michele. I lifted the lid, and there it was: the light blue shirt we had seen in the hotel boutique upon our arrival. I didn't quite know how to take that Pretty Woman moment. I called her to thank her for the gift, took a quick shower, and put on the gray shirt that I'd planned to wear all along. Needless to say, Michele had reserved the best table in the box at La Esquina de Carlos Gardel for an evening of tango. All through dinner, she continued to be unusually quiet and often looked at me with melancholic eyes, as if she expected me to say more than I said or say something different.

"You are leaving tomorrow," she said in the intermission, "so I am feeling as blue as the shirt you opted not to wear."

The show was great: the attraction of the bodies, the passion, the tug of war, the power, the fire. Life as I did not live it.

When we made it back to the hotel, she wanted to prolong the evening and have a drink, just like the day before at the golf club. I was exhausted and didn't want to make it a tradition to stay up late. In anticipation, I had begun to yawn in the car. I said, "no, thank you," "I am dead," no again, "positively not," and I kept declining her invitation all the way to the door of her room.

"Tonight I didn't get enough mileage out of you," she said.

I was surprised by her rudeness. Until that moment, she'd always treated me exquisitely, but apparently she didn't tolerate a refusal. Her comment called for a correction. There were lines.

"Good night," I replied with all the dryness I was able to muster and went into my room without looking back. Shortly, I heard Michele slam her door. Sometimes, she behaved like a capricious girl, like when she'd wanted to stop in the vineyard to "be part of the landscape," but that was the first time she'd turned against me. Not a minute had passed when the phone rang.

"I just can't believe you are leaving tomorrow," she said meekly.

"I forgive you," I broke out, knowing that she was too proud to apologize explicitly.

She tried to keep on talking, but I composed a "see you tomorrow" and hung up. I wasn't just annoyed with her burst of bad temper but also a little fed up with her steady company. As I took off my shoes, I reflected on what she'd said to me: "Not enough mileage," as if I were a car and my performance had to be measured!

The next day, breakfast started a bit roughly, but I ended up easing the tension. There was no need to punish her in excess. It wasn't all that important. The truth is that I was in a better mood because it was the last day. Our sudden farewell the night before hadn't ruined my optimism about going back home. Before leaving the breakfast room, I choked down another coffee and agreed to meet Michele half an hour later at the hotel's door, where a chauffeur would be taking me to the airport. I would spend that time walking around and saying goodbye to Buenos Aires.

I went through the hotel's revolving door and looked up at the sky. There it was, bright and blue, like a puzzle piece between the high rises of the Recoleta neighborhood.

It felt good to use those minutes to vent the array of feelings that Michele inspired in me and do some stocktaking. On the one hand, I felt grateful. The trip had been amazing, wonderful, with the best hotels, the most select restaurants, the priceless comfort of the first-class seats. A luxury certainly out of my reach. Michele had made a space for herself in my heart by genuinely always wishing the best for me. She praised my virtues. With remarks such as, "I can't stand stupidity or the lack of sense of humor," she made me feel smarter and funnier than I really am. She endorsed me and gave me security. She was truly—as she'd often claimed—always on my side. How was I not going to forgive her for last eve's unfortunate comment?

But on the other hand, Michele's personality wasn't what I'd call easy. She required a lot of attention, especially from me. In addition to being on my side, she also wanted to be *by my side*. She expected it. Always. But I didn't feel in debt to her. A few days had been enough to realize that Michele would fail in allowing my need for freedom, something I valued at least as much as her priceless emotional support. She had proven the point the day before. Sometimes, I just couldn't take spending all those long hours together, but she was oblivious to the fact that I needed my space, my own time away from her.

Michele had left the door open to new trips, and a part of me willingly accepted that possibility. I needed affection, and she gave me buckets of it, but her circumstances and mine were not the same, or where we stood in life, or everything else that mattered most to me and I had so much trouble talking about. In short, it was unfortunate that Michele was a woman. And what a woman!

There wasn't much to see near the hotel, so after enjoying alone the gentle Buenos Aires breeze for about twenty minutes, I waited for Michele at the front door. I could hear the birds chirping and the distant clamor of a lawn mower. Where could those noises come from? Undoubtedly, there was a hidden garden somewhere, but I just couldn't see it. Michele had stayed behind at the reception desk talking with the concierge about some "loose ends." That's how she referred to the silly little things that always happen when you travel and that she managed to blow out of proportion until she elevated them to the category of problems. Apparently, the orientation of the rooms did not fit her specifications. I preferred to leave her alone. After all, it was her war to fight. She would give me the summary later, all the give and take—always more take than give—until she'd win. I knew she would take her time. She enjoyed every battle. There was no stronger will on earth than hers to get her way. If she stood for something, it was determination. She had the brains too. She'd managed to convince me to cross the ocean to go with her on that trip. My role when she squabbled over something was to play good cop, but I usually just left. It hurt to see the others first trying to please her, then trying to fight her, then finally just becoming smaller and smaller until Michele, her voice always steadily calm, passed over them like a steamroller. I'd been so many times on the other side of people like her, especially when I was a salesman, that I commiserated with Michele's opponents. Why didn't she show her most human and generous side? She concentrated her love on a few people—her friend Angie and myself—and on a couple of charitable causes to which she committed much of her time. She did not mind showing everyone else a bulldog face if by doing so she got a benefit. She was like a *macaron* cookie: hard on the outside and tender inside.

The car was waiting with the luggage loaded to take me to the airport. Michele's flight didn't leave until late in the afternoon, but she had insisted on coming with me, and there was no stopping her. I guess it was a thoughtful detail, but I just wanted to be alone. I don't know how to explain it. She was like that sixth cherry. I could only take so much of her. Past a certain point, just her presence made me sick. Then I liked her again and missed her, and I only remembered all the good things she gave me.

I rested my back on a long row of flower pots overflowing with red flowers. They were not geraniums—at least not the ones I knew—but they were similar. A few feet away, two children about eight years old looked at the flowers, their eyes wide open. Out of curiosity, I got close to them. The taller of the two brought his index finger to his mouth to indicate silence, and the other pointed at one of the pots.

"It's huge," he whispered.

I couldn't remember seeing such a large butterfly before. With its wings fully open, it measured almost a handspan. You couldn't see the flower it rested on—it was that big. What could be special about that flower for the butterfly to have chosen it among so many others? They all seemed quite the same. The flower struggled to support the insect's weight, the stem swaying and bending so much that it could break at any moment. The children only had eyes for the butterfly and gazed with awe at its white wings adorned with small, button-round blue circles.

Why didn't they care about the fragility of the flower? I thought about blowing the butterfly off, but the bug flew away before I did. The children looked at me hatefully, as if it were my fault that it was gone.

"C'mon, it's just a winged caterpillar," I said to them, but they were already running down the street, watching the butterfly gracefully rise and fall in the air. Only I cared for the flower's newly recovered freedom.

"Fixed," said Michele, scaring the hell out of me. "Should we go?"

We got into the black car, sank in the back seat, and got going. Soon, the window was painted the wonderful lilac of the jacaranda trees lining up along the road. I opened the window a few inches and took a deep breath so that I could smell them, but the leather of the car's upholstery and the sandalwood notes of Michele's perfume covered their scent.

Michele was strangely quiet on our way to the airport.

"Are you ok?" I asked to break her unusual silence. She closed the neck of her black blouse a little and passed her hand over her gray pants' left leg, as if shaking off some crumbs. Then she pressed her sunglasses against her face and hid behind the lenses. It was as if we were heading to a funeral.

"Hmm," she murmured and tilted her head slightly toward me, as if she wanted to make sure, out of the corner of her eye, that I was still paying attention to her. Her lips were a more subdued orange tone than her usual red, almost the color of flesh, like Carol's dress.

"These days I've had a good time," I said.

She turned towards me a little more but still not enough to make eye contact.

"Thank you," I added.

Michele sighed deeply, making the little nacre buttons on her blouse tremble and come alive while the air filled her lungs. Then she breathed out and looked straight ahead again. Hadn't she heard me? Or maybe she had simply decided that my thanks didn't deserve an answer. I looked out the window. The city looked beautiful. Dignified and decadent. Just like Michele. At times I recognized Paris in the wide boulevards and the black slated roofs, at times it looked more like Madrid, bustling and brazen in the morning sun. Frame after frame, Buenos Aires went by fast behind the car's tinted window.

"What time is your flight?" she asked when she realized I had given up trying to start a conversation.

"At 10:15, I think." We were running late.

I had a fleeting glimpse of the expression in her eyes behind her dark lenses. There was real sorrow floating in them. What was the matter? I felt uncomfortable and somewhat irritated at her lethargy.

The car braked suddenly. Michele placed her arm in front of my chest to protect me from a possible impact against the rear of the car in front of us.

"And that?" I exclaimed when I saw the traffic jam that seemed to have come out of nowhere.

"Demonstration, sir," said the driver and blew the horn. "What do these idiots want now?" He leaned toward the steering wheel and raised his hands up to his forehead. "We are a country of *boludos*, *viste*?"

"Great," I said. "Now for sure we'll be late."

Michele looked at her watch. She continued to keep her self-absorbed, martyr attitude. The cars began to blow their horns insistently in an exasperating symphony.

"You will make it," she said, her voice as thin as paper, as if she had trouble talking.

I looked out the window again. The traffic was impossible. I shouldn't have taken so long at breakfast or I should have skipped the walk. I thought of Christine, her infectious laugh drowning in the echoes of the tango of the previous day. I imagined myself running down the runway with my suitcase open, leaving a trail of clothes on the asphalt, while the plane took off and flew away without me. I thought of my work in the cellar, of my sofa, and of my precious moments of solitude. I had to go onboard that flight to Paris. I stuck my head out the window. Some fifty yards away, a small group of people waved red banners fiercely. Why didn't they demonstrate in their frigging house?

"Stay here," Michele told me decisively. She opened the car door and headed quickly to the protesters. I made a move to follow her, but the driver turned around and said jokingly, "I wouldn't try to stop her. I think Mrs. Keller is quite capable of dealing with them by herself."

I smiled at his remark. He was totally right. It was a noisy yet peaceful gathering.

Michele walked stiffly towards the group, making her way between the stopped cars. All of the protesters were men. I saw her ask something of one of them, who pointed to the big guy holding the megaphone a few feet away. Michele took off her sunglasses. She smiled and shook hands with the husky protester. They started to talk. I guessed they used English because Michele didn't speak a word of Spanish. The man shook his head. He looked serious, almost angry. He probably was the one leading the others. Michele pointed at our car and stroked her hair. They continued chatting. After a while, both burst into laughter, and within a few seconds the big man brought the megaphone up to his lips, and the compact group began to split in two and move to both sides of the road, like Moses parting the Red Sea.

"What did I tell you?" the driver said.

Seconds later, Michele was back in the car. We started to roll again.

"You are amazing," I said. "How did you do it?"

"He has a daughter in London, and he misses her just as much as you miss Christine."

I turned around and watched the demonstrators close again behind us. Ahead of us, the road was clear. The dashed line that separated the lanes would soon be that of the runway. I focused my eyes on the asphalt and stayed in limbo—my mind already set on the next day—until I felt Michele's hand, hot and sweaty, falling like a slab on mine. I was surprised. She had never touched me, not like that, only a couple of times in the casual way friends sometimes do. Why then and in that way? Why did it come across as so intimate? I asked her with my eyes, but she was looking straight ahead. I tried to convince myself that there was innocence in that gesture, but inside me I knew that this was just a taste of what was to come. Was she beginning to demand payment for her attentions, her compliments, the wonderful trip? Why did I feel her hand as a penetration? I didn't want it there.

"Don't be paranoid. It's just a hand," I thought.

There wasn't much room to maneuver. If I took it away, I would look ungrateful, and I didn't want to appear rude. But I also didn't want to give an ambiguous impression. I hated that. Why did she have to touch me?

I was relieved to pass a sign announcing *Aerolíneas Argentinas.*

"We'll soon be at the airport," said the driver. The prelude to the resumption of my daily life. Michele took the opportunity to gently squeeze my hand. It was just like feeling her pulse, but I took it as a reaffirmation of her possession, as if she'd stuck her flag in a newly conquered territory. I wanted to remove it—I could have removed it—but I left my hand under hers. I gave in. I glared again at the road and awkwardly waited for the butterfly to take off and fly away. When I returned to Strasbourg, Michele and I kept in touch. In the beginning she took the initiative, but as time went by, I found myself more than once checking my email just to make sure I hadn't missed any of her messages or looking impatiently at my cell phone—especially at the times when I knew she was awake—hoping to see one of her WhatsApp texts pop up.

It was hard for me to push away from her. The first few times I contacted her, I resorted to some excuse, such as checking up if she was feeling better after a cold or following up on the progress of her charitable causes, but I ended up giving up pretexts to contact her. On WhatsApp I just had to type a simple "*Bonjour!*" and insert a smiley emoticon face and see how, instantly, under her name on the app came the word "typing." She always responded very quickly, as if she were waiting for me to contact her. She made me feel valued and special.

We ended up using FaceTime almost daily. Michele liked to see my face. That alone made her happy for the day, she said. She learned my routine, and even that Ecco was my favorite brand of shoes. She knew my agenda better than I did, and when we talked in the late afternoon, I was surprised that she remembered things that I'd mentioned in passing, sometimes a long time ago. She learned that François and Bernadette didn't get along as well as I'd like them to, and that the Three Musketeers were a myth. She knew of every tug of war with Samantha, and she even recommended readings for Christine and gave me advice on her sex education that I never passed on to her.

She never questioned how I felt or my motives for doing or not doing something. Little by little, I opened up to her. I could even trust her and make fun of Picard. Michele loved my imitations, and more than once we laughed together at how snooty he was. When I told her my strategies to get a raise—based on sales increase statistics—she listened to me patiently and then said.

"Numbers, numbers, numbers. You have to appeal to Picard's heart with the same passion. What does he want? What is he afraid of? Human beings are, above all, emotional creatures."

But I didn't know how to do that. I didn't know how to put feelings on a spreadsheet.

No one took as much interest as she did in discovering what mattered to me and what didn't—sometimes way too much. She prioritized anything concerning me and always made herself available. "Anything, anytime," she used to say. When I needed to vent, she became my patient listener. And the same when I was calm.

In her effort to understand me—I guess—she occasionally put on her psychologist's hat and gave me the third degree. I hated those times, and I hated her for doing that. It almost always happened after we had talked for a long time, and I was ready to hang up and continue with my routine, whatever it was. Talking to me charged her batteries. When she put her index finger next to the corner of her lips, I knew that she was warming up for her attack. Then her eyes lit up.

One Sunday afternoon when my head hurt and it was best not to cross me, she asked me:

"Why do you say you are happy when it's not true?"

Through the phone screen, she looked like the Great Inquisitor.

"I'm fine, thanks." I didn't feel like starting a debate about my happiness. She wasn't the first person to tell me, "I want you to be happy." As if I wanted to be miserable!

"Something had to happen to you," she continued, her finger so nailed to the lower part of the cheek, by her mouth, that the flesh protruded around it. "I can't understand why you live this kind of life. Not at your age." She paused. "You are at your prime."

"I'm fine, really," I insisted, raising my tone, hoping she would notice my growing disgust. I knew, based on previous experience, that she would not stop. Michele was a snowball. Once she began to roll, she grew and grew, feeding on her own comments, and knocked everything down.

"Do you have any physical impairments? Perhaps a disease?"

She frowned, which increased my perception that she was questioning me.

"Of course not. What makes you think that?" I replied, surprised that she didn't realize how much simpler the truth was.

"I would like you to trust me."

I wasn't going to fall into the trust trap. I remembered a negotiation manual that I'd read in college which devoted a whole chapter to that subject. It was as if I'd read it yesterday: "Trust is a separate issue. It is necessary to separate trust and focus the negotiation on objective issues."

"Trust has nothing to do with what I am going through or how I feel."

"I think it does." She always had to say the last word. "I could call Samantha and ask her, you know?" she threatened.

"Who do you think you are?" I thought. I felt an urge to break that finger she kept pressed close to her lips. I made a great effort to control myself and not to say things like, "Do I call your son to ask him why you never see each other? Do I ask you what you did to Dawson or Dawson to you that explains your total lack of communication? Why don't you leave me alone?"

"Go ahead," I replied calmly. I knew it was a bluff. Michele needed me, and she would never do anything to risk losing me. She knew where the boundaries that I'd set were and how far she could stretch the rope without breaking it.

"It's a free world," I challenged her. "But I am not going to give you her number."

"I can look her up," she replied undaunted. "I can ask her to friend me on Facebook. I'm sure she's curious."

"You think?"

I found she was very arrogant in trying to equate our relationship with the one between Samantha and I, even if it didn't end well. Twelve years of marriage, a daughter, and a divorce versus a few months of friendship.

Michele removed her finger from her mouth and relaxed her eyebrows.

"I won't do it because I know it would bother you."

Finally she'd said something sensible, although she'd wrapped it in an aura of condescension that I was not willing to let go. Now it was me who didn't want to drop it.

"Ask her what exactly, Michele? Say it."

She moved her head back a little, surprised that I had gone from defense to offense. She took a moment to respond.

"I have a fairly long list."

"I am sure you can give me one example."

"A marriage is always broken by something."

"Sure it is, but why are you so interested? How does that affect our friendship?" I blurted out the questions, barely catching my breath in between.

Michele looked down.

"I want to see you fulfilled, André. I want to see the best possible version of you."

"I see. Then we both want the same thing."

I looked at my watch, but I didn't notice the time.

"Oh, it's late!" I said with a half-smile.

"Not yet. You can still change."

"I'm not feeling very well." My temples were going to explode.

"Don't do it," she said. "Don't build a wall between us. Don't be on the defensive every time I ask you about this."

Wouldn't it be much easier to tell her what the issue was and put an end to everything? Why didn't I do it? The answer came quickly. I was afraid she'd treat me differently if I told her what I saw behind my eyelids when I closed my eyes. I didn't want to fall off her pedestal.

"Don't you realize that I don't want to tell you more than I've already told you?"

"But you know you could tell me anything, right? Anything. My decision about you is already made, from the very day I met you. You will always have me. I will always be on your side."

The word "always" sharpened my headache. During the first years of our marriage, Samantha had repeated the same thing to me many times. "I will always be with you. No matter what you do. Do you hear me?" she'd say, and she'd caress my cheek and lovingly bite my lips. There's no such thing as "always." Feelings change. I no longer believe whoever tells me they don't.

"Thank you for worrying," I said in a conciliatory tone. Then I remained silent. If Michele was smart—and there was no doubt she was—she would know that this pause settled the matter for the time being.

"I love you," she said.

How dare she say she loved me, just like that? What kind of love was that crazy old woman talking about? And yet, despite it all, I knew she was sincere. I believed in her love. I needed it. It repelled me, but I was so in need of it.

"Great. Thanks for loving me."

"It is true. I love you."

Something happened inside me. Nothing good.

"Talking about love, how is Dawson?"

My question didn't go down well. You could tell she was hurt. She took a long second to get her act together, but she raised her chin and answered.

"He's alright, in New York."

It was her standard response to that.

"Have you spoken with him?" I asked, deliberately touching a raw nerve.

"Not recently."

"Not recently?"

I faked sounding vaguely astonished, but we both knew that there was no hint of surprise in my question.

"No," she said in a broken voice.

"But he's okay?"

"Yes, you know, busy. New York is frantic."

She had managed to compose her voice, but her eyes looked smaller and withdrawn.

"Will you be seeing each other soon?"

"I do not know yet."

"I see."

We didn't talk for a while.

"Why are you doing this to me?" Michele said finally.

Something broke inside me when she said that.

"Sorry."

I felt as if I had shattered a vase.

"I have to hang up. I am meeting Angie for lunch."

"I'm really sorry," I repeated.

Now I was holding the pieces of the vase in my hand. I wanted to glue them together and put it back as it was before.

"I still love you," she said.

I grew very small.

"I really have to go now," she said. "One day you will know the whole story. Bye now."

Her face froze in a sad smile. Then the image disappeared, and my phone showed the home screen again. I missed her immediately despite having just talked to her and remembered something she'd said the day before:

"I'm like mold. I grow on people."

I thought of Michele rather like tonic water. Who likes it the first time? The mold suggested a messy growth, more like cancer.

"A virus, you are more like a virus," I had once told her, perhaps because my immune system was fighting her infection, causing me to suffer all kinds of reactions, some as acute as anger and frustration. Yes, sometimes Michele drove me absolutely crazy.

The truth is that my life in the months following that first trip to Argentina was never quite the same again. I guess the virus had already begun to replicate inside me, but I remained oblivious and still fooled myself and downplayed Michele's role in my life.

About three months after we'd said goodbye at the airport in Buenos Aires, she invited me on a second trip.

"Where to?"

"Wherever you want."

Michele followed a pattern, although, most likely, she was not even aware of it. First, she dropped the idea. It was always an attractive and beyond-my-reach proposition. Argentina, the world, "wherever you want." A trip was very suitable, something material and tangible that appealed to one of man's basic instincts, greed, and to a spirit of adventure that we all also have. Who is not a bit greedy? Who does not feel a slight excitement at the prospect of visiting other places and exploring other cultures? Then she let that general idea ferment so that the seed she'd planted could germinate and grow within me. After some time, she laid down the specifics and harvested.

When I shared this suspicion with Bernadette, she reproached me with something I had already been told before:

"It's kind of ugly to be so distrustful, you know? It makes you less attractive."

The first time she proposed the new trip, I said no. I'd had a good time in Mendoza, but I remembered the tense moments in the golf club or the night of the tango show. I got along better with her from a distance. In person, I had more trouble keeping her within my limits. For a few more weeks, I managed to give her the runaround, hoping she'd forget, but Michele reiterated her offer on every occasion. This time she didn't use any excuse, such as asking me to be her interpreter or something like that. That made it harder for me to accept. Without an excuse, feelings ruled. Was I starting to feel something for Michele? "Impossible," I kept saying to myself, but the truth was that my routine had already begun to gravitate around the times when we could talk.

Bernadette, needless to say, gave me her opinion.

"Do you realize that you talk about her constantly? Don't try to control everything with your head. Press the off button, will you? Do what you feel, not what you think, even if it doesn't fit your parameters. Flow. You complain about your boss, but sometimes it seems that you are the one with the stick up your ass."

She's right. I so do not flow.

"Anyway, with you it's just a matter of insisting," Bernadette reminded me. "You say, 'no' a thousand times and the one that makes it a thousand and one ..."

One night when the icy wind of loneliness was blowing hard, and the "little man" was shivering with cold, I was the one who opened the door to a new trip. I knew Michele would come to my rescue.

"It should be a warm place," I said.

"What do you think of South Africa?"

"South Africa sounds wonderful."

Wine, of all things, ended up providing us with the perfect excuse. We both liked it, and we both knew that if needed we could blame about anything on it. Michele booked adjoining rooms at a Stellenbosch resort at the foot of Groot Drakenstein Mountain. Together they formed a villa in the heart of the vineyard. The first few days were quite similar to those in Argentina, but then more disturbing ones followed.

My feelings for Michele had changed since the last time. How could they not, if they were not even the same at different times of the day. I could, during the same lunch, be torn between fascination and rejection, symbiosis and parasitism. Michele kept me on a short leash. She demanded dedication beyond reason, and although I must admit that she didn't ask for anything she wasn't willing to give me in return, I sometimes rebelled at my own inability to keep her at bay. Many times, I thought it was worth it, other times not at all. In the process, I tried to draw a line connecting the highs and the lows of the roller coaster through which my feelings traveled, hoping it would show me where they were headed. My aim was to find a general emotion that summarized the nature of our relationship, and it exasperated me not to find it.

The third night, I went out onto the terrace to get some fresh air.

During dinner, Michele had been attentive and loving, and I had been left with a kind aftertaste when we'd wished each other good night at the door of our rooms.

I rested my arms on the railing. It was wet and oily because of the night dew. The vineyard slept in front of me, and the forest closed in a little further. The air smelled damp announcing a change in the weather. Rows of clouds ran across the moon like a wildebeest's stampede. At times, the dark night lit up. The same black trees dyed silver, and when the wind rocked them in the African chiaroscuro, they sounded as if they hid a rattlesnake inside. Rain was coming.

A dim light filtered through the shutter's slats and projected in the night's thick atmosphere. Dozens of mosquitoes danced to the melody coming from Michele's adjoining terrace. It sounded like the prelude to one of those black and white films where kisses were given with hats on and heads tilted all the way back. I imagined myself in a dance hall full of thin-lipped women with wavy updos and slick-haired gentlemen dressed in their tuxedos. Maybe Chicago in the 40s. Just maybe.

I like old things. I don't know if I've said this before.

"*I'm sentimental, so I walk in the rain.*" It was Sinatra, without a doubt, who started singing as soon as the band stopped playing. "*I've got some habits even I can't explain.*"

Then, in an impossible duet, Michele's voice overlapped Sinatra's and slipped through the screen that separated our terraces.

"*Could start for the corner,*" said "The Voice" in a soul caressing whisper.

"Turn up in Spain," joined Michele with identical nostalgia, as if they were dragging together a suitcase down the same road. It turned out to be a premonition of what, months later, would end up exploding in Barcelona.

I looked out at Michele's terrace, hypnotized by that music. She was barefoot and smiley, dressed in just a pale pink blouse going down to her knees. She was rocking her waist slowly.

"Frankie?" I asked.

She looked at me as if she'd been waiting for me. She lowered her eyelids and continued rocking to the rhythm of the music.

"No one like him," she said.

I took off my shoes and jumped over to her terrace. There was some reproach in that display of agility. I still had something she would never have again: a pinch of youth.

"Why try to change me now," Michele sang, stopping at each word, as if that was the most important message of the song's lyrics, what she wanted me to grasp.

"That was me," she said as the music continued to play. "Always willing to jump in the deep end."

"Too late for you to change?" I asked.

"Shh. Listen," she replied, and moved her index finger from her mouth to her ear.

Why can't I be more conventional?
People talk
People stare
So I try
But can't be.

At each line she moved her head from side to side. I didn't know whether she was denying the message or denying herself. Most likely, neither one. She was delighted with the lyrics. That song was a compendium of her life. All of a sudden, a violent gust of wind blew, and the trees bent, unleashing their rattling. Michele shivered and hugged herself as if she were cold, but I thought she was scared rather than cold, afraid that perhaps the wind would blow the notes of her song to the depths of the forest. Meanwhile, I was intrigued.

"The evening is turning," I said.

I looked up where the moon had been, but there was no sign of it. The sky looked brown where the light coming out of the rooms met the clouds.

"I agree. Scared?" she said.

The first drops of rain fell on my head, then on my feet. They were cold. Soon, the teak flooring was flecked with black circles.

"It's just a big cloud," I said as I moved closer to her. "It'll pass."

"Then dance," she whispered in a tone halfway between an invitation and a command.

Dance? I couldn't remember the last time I'd danced: at my wedding, maybe? But then I wasn't wearing pajamas.

Her gaze was both challenging and encouraging, like that of a mother who is teaching her son how to swim.

"Are you going to leave me dancing alone?"

I took her by the waist and began to swing timidly, my feet anchored to the floor. Something inside me asked me to dance but my legs didn't obey. At the touch of my hands, she smiled. I bent down a little. I didn't want her to feel short, although barefoot she seemed to have shrunk since dinner. She ran her hands behind my head and whispered the lyrics in my ear. Michele was singing to me.

"So let people wonder, let 'em laugh, let 'em frown ..." she said, gently pressing the back of my neck. "You know I'll love you ..." She opened her eyes, her look so far removed from the arrogance I'd seen her use with other people so many times before."... Till the moon's upside down."

"Is the moon really upside down or are we?" I asked.

She pushed me away a little and threw her head back. In the dim light, she looked younger and, for a moment, anything seemed possible.

"It's raining!" she said, as if the rain was wonderful, and I hadn't noticed that our feet were getting totally wet.

I removed a strand of hair from her eyes. It was beginning to frizz with the rain, and I knew she didn't like her hair curly.

"If there is something I don't want to change, it's you," she whispered, as if that was part of the song.

But when I tuned my ear to hear Frank Sinatra repeat that, the lyrics kept saying:

Why try to change me, why try to change me now.

"Don't you think it's amazing?" Michele asked me. Her cheek rested now on my chest. "You and me. Two sentimentalists, walking in the rain."

"Perhaps we'll end up in Spain."

"I am soaked!" she shouted and burst into laughter.

Her bangs were wet, crushed over her forehead.

"I guess it's time to stop dancing."

"Just wait a second," she said and pressed herself to me. "Wait until the song is over."

I closed my eyes. Time diluted. As the rain climbed up my pants, I accepted that I could never free the mosquito without ruining the amber and decided to take Michele as she was: wonderful.

When the song was over, she said she was cold and headed to her room. When she reached the door, she turned around and smiled at me, and I followed her into her room, fully aware that I was venturing into the lion's den but also trusting my taming skills.

That night Michele and I inaugurated a new routine in our schizophrenic relationship. We hugged and caressed over our clothes, as if we wanted to cover with our hands the cracks in our souls. There was no sex; no kissing; I didn't even see her skin below her pink blouse, and yet it was undoubtedly intimate and real. If you feel something, then it exists.

I didn't stay too long, but half an hour was long enough to realize that I hadn't taken an inconsequential step. My need for affection and physical contact laid my extreme fragility bare. As a result, receiving Michele's caresses or giving them to her didn't soothe me. I had moved from anorexia to bulimia, and now I just wanted to vomit. I felt guilty for having fed on a food different than the one I really craved. Why had I done it? Was I so hungry for love?

I went back to my room with the added concern of how to stop this new trend. Knowing Michele, it would be virtually impossible to go back. Once she conquered a new land, it was scorched earth. She would seek to build that "hugging time" into our routine, as she had done with the after-dinner drink that had led to our fight in Buenos Aires. When you gave her something she liked once, she wanted it in increasing doses.

Michele was a love junkie. And me? What was I?

The next morning, I struggled to keep my distance and reverse the situation. I behaved as if nothing had happened after dinner: the dance, the caresses, the regrets. If we didn't talk about it, it would be as if it hadn't happened, I thought with remarkable naivety, ignoring that Michele wouldn't show any willingness to relegate the events of the day before into oblivion.

"Last night was very comforting," she told me before breakfast was over. I didn't answer, so she insisted:

"And for you?"

"Comforting, yes," I acknowledged before I started to talk about the plans for the day, which otherwise went according to the usual canons. We had been invited to a barbecue on a farm in the countryside. Our host, Garth, received us on the back of a horse as black as Portento. Just before lunch, he briefed us on the different types of meat cuts. Then, under a vine arbor, we ate more beef than we could handle. Hadn't we attended a similar event in Argentina? A couple of times, I caught Michele looking at me as if she wanted to read my mind. I wouldn't let her. Although sometimes my emotions came to the surface with extreme ease, I'd been hiding others for so long that I'd become an expert at putting on a poker face if the situation called for it. Michele, impatient by nature, had at the same time the gift of opportunity. In other words, she dominated the tempo. She knew how to wait, despite hating it, for the right moment to throw in an invitation or just a suggestion, and when to keep quiet and let things unfold naturally.

That night we decided to retire just after our dinner at the hotel restaurant. We had managed to finish a bottle of De Toren Fusion V, and when we got to our villa I was laughing in a lazy, silly way. My intention was to wish her goodnight at the door of her room, so when the moment came, I said, "Good evening" and looked in my pocket for my key card. Michele ignored my farewell, set one foot in her room, and turned around:

"Are you coming in?"

That very same André who in Argentina had kept his hand under hers, the one who changes his course like a weather vane and sometimes loses his way, agreed again to spend time with Michele, a time which wasn't exactly sexual, but definitely sensual. I don't like that André. That's why I'm talking about him in the third person, à la Bernadette.

That became our routine the following nights, except one when I refused to go into her room to stand up for some forgotten principle. Michele avoided fighting back as she'd learned not to since Buenos Aires. We always met in her room—that way it was me who chose when to leave—and went on with our pseudo chaste ritual that one part of me judged sick and the other, therapeutic. I really couldn't say if I did it for her or to give voice to a vital despair that I couldn't name. On our last night in South Africa, Michele named it for me.

She sat on the sofa, a meadow of huge garnet flowers. She crossed her legs, and her knee came out through the slit of the skirt, then the entire calf, as pale as an image of the virgin I had once seen in a procession in Zamora, and finally the long, narrow, oscillating foot, her toenails painted a cobalt blue. She looked at me with big eyes and a short smile—that combination, I'd learned, meant that she was ready for me—and I dropped on the sofa next to her, taking care not to sit on the gap between the two seats. Although the distance was short and only that minimal soft chasm separated us, I was aware that this closeness was only possible in the confines of a room with the blinds down, or the drapes closed, or in a villa in the countryside, like that one, far from any windows other than our own.

She took her glass from the table and handed me mine. She left it almost floating in the air, just as she'd done with her hand the day we'd met in the offices of Junot Cellars, and I took it, brushing her pinky in the exchange. That finger, so fragile for such a formidable woman, showed she was, after all, a mortal like me. Then she drank. We drank. She took one sip, I took two, of a Cobblers Hill that we'd bought in the morning. Then I rested the back of my neck on her chest, and time diluted, our ages dissipating in the gloom of the room. In the light of the sliver of moon reflecting through the window, you couldn't see the strange bird on the tapestry hanging above the fireplace or tell the age of the watchful ladies in the portraits. On one wall, there were oil paintings of former European queens and opposite them, colorful watercolors of ebony women.

"Would you hug me?" she said softly.

The fan circled above our heads, stirring the chocolate-thick air with its wooden blades.

I was surprised that she'd even asked me. It was understood. After all, it wasn't our first evening on that sofa that week. What was different that night? Why did she ask me instead of waiting for me to offer? What was the longing? Why the rush? I put my arm behind her neck. She was perspiring.

I leaned back against her beating heart, careful not to spill the wine.

"Am I hurting you?" Her chest felt like jelly under the red blouse.

"Most of the time, you don't," she said, and gave herself ample time before continuing. "You are a good man."

I made a wry face. Was I? Was I really a good man?

"Tired?" I asked.

"Strangely, I am not. It has been a long day, but I don't want it to end."

I caressed her forearm. Her skin opened under my fingers as the dry land opens to the plow. Michele caressed my chest, sliding her hand gently over my torso. I closed my eyes and listened to her heartbeat just as I remembered hearing the sea inside the conch. I imagined the waves breaking gently between my legs. I felt the beginning of an erection. I bent my knees. Would she have noticed?

"What a couple we make," she said.

I left the glass on the carpeted floor. There were two of us, but I resisted the idea that we were a couple the way she'd hinted.

"A weird one," I said.

"Oh, no, no, not weird," she hastened to refute. "Unique, if anything."

"Unique sounds better, but we are weird, Michele. Weird."

Or was it not weird to feel my crotch get tighter at the touch of an old woman?

Right away, I thought I'd betrayed Michele by thinking of her as an old woman. She couldn't have read my mind—it'd been easier to notice my erection—and yet I felt as guilty as though I'd said it aloud. I'd attacked her at her most vulnerable spot, perhaps the only one she had no control of, for time goes by, inexorably, for everyone. I shook my head to scare those thoughts away, and deep inside I apologized to her while feeling the increasing pressure in my pants. What would happen if I grabbed her hand and moved it a little further down, right where my belly triangulated? What would she do? Would she continue to go lower? Would she back away? Something told me she would not. And if she didn't stop, would I like it? What would come next? I looked fleetingly between my legs and allowed myself a few moments of introspection. Michele was quiet now, and her silence was complicit with my fantasy. I imagined her naked, and then I remembered Pauline, the last woman I had tried to have sex with in that little hotel on the beach in Arcachon. The sight of her youthful nakedness replaced Michele's.

Pauline had been my last attempt at deceiving somebody, primarily myself, shortly after going soft with Antoinette. It was a crude, coarse, explicit memory: her rubbing against my cock, trying to make it hard, calling my name between fake moans. To try to satisfy Pauline, I ended up drinking the broth of my own humiliation. Pauline was an affectionate girl with mahogany curls, a friend of a friend—as if that was a guarantee of anything—with an apple ass and perfect breasts, neither big nor small, which fit just perfectly in my hand. Pauline kissed well, giving long, sweet kisses. In a corner on the way to the hotel, we stopped to lick each other like teenagers. She looked at me with a sparkle in her eyes beyond that moment, beyond desire. How I hated being looked at like that! I knew there was no future. "You know how to kiss," Pauline told me and pressed her hips against mine, not knowing that I was a fraud, before her illusion and my lie, two sides of the same coin, were diluted at the first contact with the bed sheets. "Are you this good at everything else?" she whispered with a knowing smile, and she bit my lips in the dim light of the lamppost. After Pauline, I didn't try again. What for. I already knew that this was not my way. How could Michele, at sixty-five, resurrect those buried passions? I looked out the window. The moon had climbed to the corner. The sight of something real, like the moon, brought me back to the sofa. I left Michele's hand where it was, resting on my chest. The fragile balance of our relationship rested on not going below the navel.

"What we have is rare, not weird," she said. "It is only unexplored territory."

"I'm sorry but no," I said sharply. "If I could get out of myself and see us from above, I would think this is weird, Michele. Not unique. Not special. Not sublime. Not rare. Weird."

A desolate silence followed my words. I put my hand on hers. Her hand was just laying there. It had stopped caressing my chest. I couldn't feel her pulse, but it was warm, yes, it was warm.

"But I can't get out of myself," I added, hoping to make her feel better. "I can't forget who I am."

The blades turned. They hadn't stopped turning, but only then was I aware of their movement. They went round and round. A punch in the gut told me I shouldn't have said anything. Maybe there was nothing wrong with letting Michele live her fantasy. The air had thickened and was so dense that you could see it.

"What color are roses?" Michele asked me when the air and the silence were one and the same.

"What roses?" I whispered, somewhat surprised by her question. There were no flowers in the room in Arcachon from where my mind had not yet completely returned or in that one in Stellenbosch, just a crack in the roof's corner and Pauline's back hunched by my side, as still as Michele's hand.

"Any."

Michele covered my lips with two fingers. I was relieved to feel that they had moved.

"Wait," she added. "Don't rush to answer."

I smiled. When I moved my lips, I noticed the aftertaste of the wine on the sides of my mouth and under my tongue.

"Were you going to say red?", she asked.

"I was going to say white," I replied just to contradict her.

Michele gently slapped me on the cheek and let time pass. I wondered what roses had to do with the nature of our relationship. Sometimes, she chose an image without any apparent link with the subject of the conversation—a flower as in this case, a Venice flooded by high water, or those tunnels resulting from the delusions of some Maginot—and then used it to emphasize her point. I waited for her to continue to see where she was going. I would decide then whether I'd go with her or not.

"Have you ever heard of Halfeti's roses?" she said at last.

I shook my head. Michele caressed my beard with the same fingers that she'd just used to silence my answer.

"Halfeti is a small town in Turkey, where these black roses grow." She looked at me to measure my reaction. I struggled not to show any.

"These are some unique roses."

"Call me classic, but I prefer them red. Or white."

"These are the only ones in the entire world, and they can only exist there, in Halfeti."

"Really?" I tried to sound casual, but it came out louder than I'd intended, showing a bit of impatience. I was starting to see which way the wind was blowing.

"They are actually born as red as the rest," she said to appease me, "but apparently the soil is rich in a substance ... what's it called? Now I can't think of the name, but it is the same one which gives blueberries their dark color. That compound, together with the groundwater that seeps from the Euphrates, causes red to turn black in the winter months. And that makes them unique."

I shrugged.

"Therefore, Halfeti roses are special, rare, but not weird. Because they exist in nature like you and I exist at this time, on this sofa."

"Touché," I said and reached for my glass.

"And I assure you, André, my dear, that I have never in my life seen more beautiful roses than these I am talking about."

Overall, I liked to listen to Michele, although sometimes she went in circles. She always found a beautiful way to make the anomalous sound extraordinary.

"The way you say it, it doesn't sound so bad."

"This thing we have is not so strange after all," she said, resuming her original thought line. "It's just a path that neither one of us has walked before. There are no rules because we are writing them as we go along. *You* write the rules."

I liked her philosophy, the freedom of it—a new, unexplored world, a blank book without any pages dedicated to some Pauline or Antoinette. And above all, a sexless, failure-free world, one where love was possible beyond the expectation of winding up between the sheets. The age difference made it unthinkable. I closed my eyes. My groin didn't hurt anymore, and Pauline was a fuzzy memory.

Black roses. Suddenly, they looked to me like the most sublime flowers. I decided right then that one day I'd visit Halfeti, in winter if possible, in time to see the roses turn from red to the dark color of blueberries.

"Don't wait," I thought I heard her say, her voice as thin as a spider's web, but it may very well be that she didn't say anything at all.

A shiver ran down my arm, and all my tranquility fell like dry dust on the carpet.

"Are you ok?" I asked. I sat up on the sofa. Michele was paler than usual and sweating. She looked like a burnt-out candle.

"Yes," she hesitated. "It's this heat. I don't understand the lack of air conditioning."

I took her hand and squeezed it gently.

"Michele ..."

It was unusual to see her with scared little mouse eyes.

“It’s reassuring to have you here,” she said.
“Good to know because I’m not going anywhere.”
Something was wrong, but I did not know what yet.

ANDRÉ

FRIDAY

The trip to New York was as long and tedious as expected, especially when you add in a sticky folding table and a musty smelling cabin to the usual lack of legroom. What happened to the days when flying was glamorous? Michele had gotten me used to finer things. To tell the truth, she'd sent me enough money to make the journey in Business, but I couldn't overcome my own class consciousness, so I ended up flying Economy. Once I went through the nasty immigration inspection, my red eyes, furry mouth, and the rest of what was left of me were immediately met by a large sign reading, "Welcome to the United States." Did I do that too, say one thing and do another? I walked down the corridor that led to the baggage claim area, hoping that this lonely and uncomfortable trip would make some sense and that the risk of Michele's mark on me turning into an ugly scar was worth taking.

Too late for these considerations. I was already in New York City.

As soon as I had my suitcase, I put Michele on the back burner. I was to meet Lucy in the airport terminal. My mind was busy revisiting a long string of shared youthful memories, when we both peeked into adulthood with laughter, and there was no room for anything too serious. I remembered the afternoons in the park and Jacques's famous party. That's where we hooked up in the bathroom, and she showed me the four-leaf clover she had tattooed on her butt. She almost convinced me to get a macaw tattooed that night! How silly. Luckily, I didn't. Everyone would have known the next morning. Keeping secrets was never her forte. Lucy's parents were Spanish, and her real name was Lucía, but for us, her friends, she was always Lucy. It was as if we sensed that one day she'd cross the ocean and settle in the USA. I was now trying to make my way through the arrivals terminal between two obese police officers dragging their feet. One was eating a donut; the other was holding a gigantic coffee. They looked around suspiciously, seeming both ridiculous and scary. It had just occurred to me that their absurdity was somewhat macabre when I felt a strong grip on the back of my shoulder. Scared, I released the handle of my suitcase which slammed onto the floor. A crowd of students nearby looked up from their cell phones. One of the policemen took the donut out of his mouth as if it had suddenly turned stale, while the other rapidly moved his hand to his gun. Were they looking at me?

"This is no country for handsome Frenchmen," said a voice behind me.

My heart skipped a beat. I turned around, and there was Lucy with the same Minnie Mouse smile she had when we were twenty years old. She had frightened me. Only a few wrinkles around her violet eyes showed that many years had passed. It was so good to see her again.

She first hung from my neck, hugged me tightly, and then kissed me under the ear and whispered, "Welcome to New York." This time, coming from Lucy, I believed it.

"You look the same! How are you? How exciting!" I strung all three together.

"No, you look the same. Well, no, you look better!"

I backed up a little and grabbed her hands. I looked her over from top to bottom. "Lucy ..." She'd kept every curve of her five-foot, three-inch body. Her one size too small Gap sweatshirt fit tightly over her breasts advertising her voluptuous hourglass body. She was the same and yet she was different. Those teenage clothes concealed the passage of time quite well. I was first date nervous and probably a little shaky, but I don't think that she could tell. This meeting was in many ways brand new. Twenty-two years had gone by since Lucy initiated me in the back seat of a yellow Peugeot. I remembered every bit of it. She did everything. I just provided the car—actually, my mother had reluctantly lent it to me. And yet, despite all those years, there was more left than anyone would think of that young man who was struggling to be an adult in the darkness of that desolate parking lot.

"Thank you for coming," I said. "Where did you leave the car?"

Lucy's car had seats on the sides, bars to the ceiling and hanging straps. It smelled of hot dogs and cost $2.75. She had come on the subway.

"You really look good," she kept saying on our way to her place. "Do you want us to go out tonight? It's Friday."

I had no desire to go party, but she overcame my reluctance with a charming look and a simple "Come on." How could I resist?

Lucy lived in a fifth-floor walkup on 132nd Street. It could have been worse because it was a seven-story brownstone.

"Welcome to the *Upper* Upper East Side," she said with a smile as we left the subway station. "Harlem for everybody else."

I liked the neighborhood—right where Manhattan lost its luster but before the Big Apple showed its worm. I felt at ease in these border territories, probably, but not only, a consequence of being Alsatian.

Making eye contact with men and women of all races and conditions, in that corner of America, shook off my drowsiness and awakened my curiosity. I was in New York, where anything was possible. I almost forgot that I was there to do Michele one last favor.

"What if I just don't do it?" I said out loud. I was sitting on the sofa I was going to sleep on. "What if don't go see John?"

"What if I kick you in the ass?" Lucy said. Then we spent a long time catching up.

"Do you feel like going to a drag queen show?" she suggested.

The idea annoyed me, but I replied that I would love to with remarkable enthusiasm.

"My best friend will be joining us," she said cheerfully. "His name is Tony. You'll see, you'll adore him."

"Of course I will."

"I mean my best friend here," she added and patted my leg. I pulled her earlobe affectionately.

"He's swishier than the drag queens themselves," she said, "but he has a heart of gold."

"The more the merrier," I struggled to say. "New York, here we come!"

Honestly, I would have preferred a quieter evening. We hadn't seen each other for so many years! Ten? Fifteen? The last time was at her father's funeral. On the plane, I had imagined a candlelight dinner in one of those small Italian restaurants with a red and white checked tablecloth, a pot with a single flower and a fresh clover—that I added just because—some Fettuccine Alfredo and Chicken Marsala, a jug of Lambrusco, and Sicilian cannoli that is impossible to break into two halves. After dinner, we'd have an amaretto with three ice cubes. I even half dreamed that I went back to the days of easy Peugeot sex, when laughter counted considerably more than orgasms, as if what worked then would work now. Just ask Antoinette. Reality was different. As it turned out, candles were banned in New York restaurants because they are a fire hazard, and clovers do not grow in polystyrene. But it was still nice to dream on that plane that I could set the clock back to my twenties and dream for a short time that I wasn't different, or a coward, or me.

After tea, Lucy told me she had to run some errands. I knew it was her way to leave me alone so that I could take a nap before going out. I took off my shoes and laid down on the sofa. If it wasn't for the English echo of the neighbor's radio, I could be anywhere. Then I must have fallen asleep.

At about 7:00, we jumped into a taxi to meet Tony. I had seen these yellow taxis a million times on TV and now I was inside one. The cab driver was Sikh and wore a turban, like in the movies. I watched the thousands of people hurriedly walking up and down Broadway, chasing their dreams. Was there enough happiness in the world for everyone?

The taxi stopped at a traffic light next to a sex shop. Lucy stared pensively at the red sign, the black door, and the rickety condom machine next to the entrance.

"You'll love Tony. Don't be fooled by his flamboyance. He's an activist and a truly committed guy."

"And what does he advocate for?"

"The rights of people with AIDS."

The cab moved again. I wanted to ask her if Tony had AIDS, but I thought that it was too personal a question. I just kept looking silently out the window at the procession of 7 Elevens and Dunkin' Donuts where all these dreamers fattened their frustrations.

"When you get the short straw ..." Lucy continued. Was she implying that Tony was HIV positive? I gave her a disapproving look followed by a warm smile. It didn't seem right to talk about this.

"Luckily, people no longer die of this," she concluded as the taxi stopped. "Look at him; there he is. Isn't he cute?" she said as she made a fuss through the glass.

As soon as Lucy and I got out of the cab, Tony unfurled his tail like a peacock.

"You were right. Your friend is very handsome," Tony said, and since he looked at me when he kissed Lucy, I felt kissed as well.

"I told you," Lucy said, and looked at me out of the corner of her eye.

"It's been a lifelong wait," Tony said, shaking my hand. It felt like catching a fish, all wet and slippery. "But it was worth it," he added, so close that I felt his breath caressing my ear.

Lucy pinched his ass.

"Remember that André is mine, so don't even touch him," she said winking at me. Then she grabbed each of us by one arm and we walked together the 50 feet to the door of the club. Luxurious neon marked the entrance: "Pink Velvet." What a tacky name.

I wasn't in the mood for someone like Tony, who represented everything that bothered me about the gay scene. If such a world existed, I certainly didn't want citizenship. Part of the problem lay in my vision of what it meant to be gay. It didn't have to be superficial or promiscuous. Also, I was exhausted. I'd had maybe an hour's sleep at Lucy's. She was beaming and eager to have a good time. She had pulled her hair up in a bun and spread glittery makeup on her face and neckline. The effect was simply dazzling. The Gap girl who'd picked me up at the airport had vanished.

The Pink Velvet was in a basement. The first flight of stairs ended in front of a pink velvet curtain—clever—guarded by a black drag queen behind a rosebud-shaped shiny jet-black booth. The color contrast was spectacular. The 6'5" drag queen was dressed in a wide legged, open on the sides leather jumpsuit. Chewing gum pink horns stuck out of his Afro.

"Hello guys," he said in a thundering voice. He kissed Tony on the lips and whispered something in his ear. They laughed. He touched his horns and squeezed them as if milking a cow. Then he leaned forward from behind the counter to kiss Lucy on the cheek. When he was about to leave his booth and greet me, I reached out to shake hands and prevent any kissy-kissy attempt.

"How serious," he said, pinching my cheek. "Anyway, Welcome to Pink Velvet!" he broke out shrilly, as if "well" and "come" were two separate words. He pulled the curtain open in a single movement and the three of us followed Penelope—which apparently was his name—into the club to the rhythm of the Y-M-C-A song. Tony grabbed Lucy by her waist, "locomotive style" and I followed a couple of steps behind, feeling embarrassed but also guilty for not letting myself go. Why couldn't I let my hair down for once?

Both the ambience and the music were from the 70's, the songs of my infancy. Mirror balls hung from the ceiling, and their tiny crystal squares reflected the moving spotlights and projected blotches of light onto the empty stage, around which the tables were arranged as in an amphitheater. It was jam-packed, except for a private booth for four just next to the stage. "I hope it's not ours," I thought, remembering my total embarrassment on a previous theatre soirée, a long time ago. That time my seat was by the alley, and I was taken onstage in a magic show.

"You are the boss," Lucy told Tony when Penelope had us sit at that table. "Isn't it great, André? We have the best seat in the house!"

I forced a smile and took a seat next to Lucy. Tony sat in front of me across the narrow table. There was little space, so he was very close. For the first time, I took some time to analyze his features hoping they could tell me something about his past. He was tall and thin—too thin—with prominent cheekbones and sunken cheeks. Had it not been for his jacket, all you'd see is bones. A wild, primitive aura surrounded him, and yet he was sleek, his hair slicked back, his lips thin and moist, his slanted eyes of a blue so dark that they may as well have been black.

"I know what I want to eat today," said Tony. He gave me a mischievous smile and picked up the menu. "I'm hoping for large portions. I'm starving."

"Is it a fixed menu?" I asked.

"It is, but within each column there are several options to choose from. You see?" Tony indicated on my menu what he meant, while deliberately stroking my hand. "I recommend the foie gras sausage with quail eggs," he added. "You'll lick ... your fingers."

Lucy split her sides laughing until her nose started to run, at which point she covered it with a napkin while hurriedly searching for a Kleenex inside her bag. Tears came to her eyes at a joke that I didn't find at all funny. How old were we? Fifteen? She finally excused herself and ran to the bathroom. As soon as Lucy left, Tony got serious, as if he'd been acting until then and was now removing his mask. I shifted in my chair. Maybe I'd been a little rude keeping so quiet. I looked for something to say to break the ice, but he spoke first.

"We're going to have fun, right?" he said, his comment sounding like a warning. "Lucy is having a hard time," he continued. "I want her to enjoy these days as much as possible before she starts with her sessions."

I had no idea what he was talking about. What sessions?

"You don't have to like me," he added. Suddenly, he didn't seem effeminate. "If this isn't your idea of a good time, just keep it to yourself, will you? Lucy is very sensitive to these things."

Tony smiled. He had a beautiful smile, so perfect that it could be fake.

"Stop looking miserable. Laugh. You are in the most exciting city in the world. Enjoy it!"

He gently patted my hand. His hand was warm and no longer wet. I looked down, a little ashamed. Was it really all that obvious that I didn't want to be there?

"It's the jetlag, I know," he said to ease the tension. "It's horrifying, but nothing a good gin & tonic can't fix."

"Two gin & tonics, then," I said, addressing a gorgeous waiter in a white tuxedo who was just walking by our table.

I was about to ask Tony if there was something wrong with Lucy when I realized she was practically back at the table, her shoulders dancing up and down. What had Tony meant? To me, she looked the same as always.

"Did you guys order?" she said as she sat down.

"Three Bombay gin & tonics, please. They're on me!" I said.

"Make them happy ones," Tony said to the waiter's slight surprise.

"Yes, very happy ones," I repeated, and sealed a pact with Tony.

Tony was somewhat right, so I decided to have the best possible time that night, despite the dismal forecast he'd just let fly. "Sessions ..." It was virtually impossible not to tag on "chemotherapy" at the beginning, but it didn't have to be that way. Her sessions could be with a psychologist, or rehab—hadn't she mentioned that her back hurt?—even yoga or Tai Chi, but then Tony wouldn't have gotten so serious—more than serious, firm. Was she sick? I would ask her at the right time. I had to know. Why hadn't she told me? I took a deep breath. I had to change my way of thinking. I knew me enough to know that compounding negative thoughts didn't do me any good. There was no need to always assume the worst-case scenario. I looked at Lucy. She was playing with her cell phone. I didn't notice anything strange about her. Quite the opposite. She looked beautiful in her red silk blouse, unbuttoned to just above the point where your eyes fell down the cliff. Yes, she looked great, but sometimes the worst diseases are invisible on the outside. "Look at Tony," I thought, "so handsome. So sexy. No one would think he was sick."

"What are you staring at?" Lucy said, bringing me back to the Pink Velvet. "I know, I'm totally hooked on my cell phone. I won't look at it again, I promise."

I took her hand and smiled tenderly at her.

"What happened? Did I miss something when I was in the powder room?"

"I made a pass at André and he turned me down." Tony sighed.

"Stop corrupting him," Lucy said jokingly. "You won't have any luck in that department. I know because I've tried him." She grasped my hand and whispered, "Do you remember?"

"How could I forget my first time?" I thought just as the lights dimmed, and the room got almost completely dark. "Especially if it's in a yellow Peugeot." I smiled at the awkward memory. A wave of artificial smoke emerged from the sides of the stage and enveloped our table in a thick fog. The music ceased; conversations died down; expectation built up. The show was about to begin.

I must have been thinking out loud because Lucy replied, "Are you sure it was yellow?"

We both knew she hadn't forgotten.

"Canary yellow," I said.

"Do you still have that freckle on your shoulder? I was so crazy about that freckle."

"If it didn't fall off ..."

"If one day it does, send it over by UPS. I'll keep it under my pillow."

"I think I'm not needed here," Tony interrupted. He took a sip of his gin & tonic and looked at us from behind the glass.

"Of course you are, fool," said Lucy laughing.

Then I noticed a hand on my knee, under the tablecloth. I gave Lucy a knowing look, but she was unfolding her napkin with both hands. Tony's hand rested so unjustifiably on my kneecap that the situation called for a strong reaction. Instead, I did nothing, envying his bravery and getting turned on at the gentle tickle of that unexpected butterfly.

"Are you sure I'm needed?" Tony insisted while stroking my knee.

An electric current ran between my legs. It was the beginning of an erection.

"You are very needed," I said.

I put my hand on his. I couldn't believe what I'd just done. "If only Lucy knew," I thought. "Lucy is going to know," was my next thought, "Tony is going to tell her."

"Should we make a threesome?" Tony said, tightly lacing his fingers with mine.

"Tony! You are going to scare André!"

"Maybe not a threesome," I thought, wishing that Tony's hand went up my leg. I was so into the game that I felt like a complete idiot when he let go of my fingers, just like that. He dropped me and quit the game.

"It's too bad you're straight," he added with a defiant look. Then he caught the waiter's attention by waving his provocative hand in the air.

I did what I could to carry on the conversation for two or three more minutes and hide my anger and frustration, but I am not completely sure I succeeded because a couple of times Lucy looked at me as if she didn't recognize me. When it no longer looked awkward, I stood up and headed to the bathroom. What for, I didn't know—to cry, to masturbate, or maybe just to bang my head against the wall. I took advantage of the hectic coming on the scene of Electra, Magnesia, and Susie, three hunks dressed in ABBA costumes. "Susie really doesn't go well with the other two," I thought as I went down the ramp to the men's room to the rhythm of "Dancing Queen." I decided she'd been added at the last minute, because she was a little shorter than her partners and her costume was less elaborate. Was I playing the part of Susie that evening?

I needed to be alone for a while to reset and analyze what had happened and what to do next. The bathroom was sometimes my sanctuary in cases like this. The men's room walls in the Pink Velvet were tiled with small, shiny black squares. Above each urinal hung a niche with a brightly colored plaster image of a saint—only it wasn't a saint; it was more like those Japanese manga figures. Did I really have to piss in front of these miniature drag queen dolls? I guess so. "What a rough start for my first night," I thought as I unzipped. I'd been such an idiot! Even though initially I'd acted a bit rudely, I still didn't deserve Tony blowing me off, especially after the gin & tonic pact. How silly I'd been letting go like that, showing all my vulnerability. As for Tony, what had he wanted to prove? How easy it was to get me horny? That he was smarter than me? Right now, he'd be laughing, possibly telling Lucy how simple it was to seduce her friend and that I was so in need of sex as to throw myself into the arms of the first guy who touched my knee under the table.

The door opened behind me, and the music slipped into the bathroom. Then the noise dimmed again. I was so deep in thought that I maybe heard a faucet run and then a few steps.

"It seems that the gin & tonic is a diuretic," Tony said from the adjacent urinal. He'd said it casually, but my plumbing shut down.

"Are you having fun?" I replied while hurriedly hiding my penis.

"At times," he said, "but we could be having a much better time, don't you think?"

Was he making a pass at me after cutting me off? Since I didn't want him to be under the impression that my ability to pee depended on his presence or absence, I still stood there for a while.

"What's Lucy up to?" I asked.

"Greeting some friends. It's a small world."

I flushed, pulled up my fly, and turned toward the sink. I looked around, as it would have been comforting to see someone else in the bathroom, but it was just the two of us.

"So you have a secret?" said Tony.

I could see his neck, his back, and his ass in the mirror.

I turned on the faucet.

"It's not a secret," I said.

"But Lucy doesn't know," he said, buttoning his pants up.

No, Lucy didn't know, but I'd been thinking all day how to tell her. I splashed water in my red, itchy eyes. When I opened them again, Tony's face was in the mirror. He was just a couple of feet behind me.

"I like you. I like you a lot," he said, taking a small step forward. He was so close he could almost touch me.

My pulse accelerated. I splashed more water on my face.

"I'm not going to eat you, you know," he said. "Not unless you want me to."

"What was really your point earlier?" I asked.

He laughed. "None, it was just a game," he said and ran his index finger across my neck.

I gazed at him with both anger and excitement. Clearly, we were playing different games. All this meant nothing to him.

He stood next to me. He was looking at his reflection and combing his eyebrows.

"I think you have to fuck more, honey," he said. "You'd feel much better."

The word "honey" hit me like a lick on my face, wet like his slippery handshake. I felt uneasy, partly with myself, and there was that crazy pressure in my pants again.

"Others apparently have fucked too much or too casually," I snapped, instantly regretting what I'd just said. It wasn't even what I thought, but it was too late to take it back. To top it off, I'd betrayed Lucy.

For a few seconds, only the splashing of the water and the rumbling of the music filled the air.

"You would have given me a blowjob, and you know it," Tony said calmly. "Do yourself a favor and fix your upstairs."

Then he left the bathroom, leaving me alone with my pathetic reflection in the mirror. Two seconds later, I followed him. The conversation wasn't over for me. I wanted to ask him about Lucy.

How could I have engaged in a fight when the important thing was to know whether my friend was sick?

"Wait!" I yelled as we walked back to the table. I was on his heels, but he didn't stop. He walked fast, avoiding the beams of light that ran through the gloom of the room like lanterns looking for a fugitive. Then I heard a drum roll, like in the circus. We were just a few steps away from Lucy. She was already greeting us with dancing fingers when I grabbed him by the shoulder and turned him around. At that moment, a flash blinded me, and everything turned white. I covered my eyes with the palms of my hands. Then I was lifted off the floor to resounding applause. When I was returned to the floor, I was overwhelmed by the stench of a perfume of a thousand flowers, and immediately, I felt two tight kisses on my cheeks. I took my hands off my eyes: Electra? I turned my head to one side. Tony looked as baffled as I did. It took me a while to realize that we were both onstage. Magnesia ran her hands over my chest while Susie covered Tony's eyes with a scarf.

"What an ideal couple we have here!" Electra announced loudly and handed me the microphone. "Bring it closer to your mouth, so we can hear you."

I was still stunned and disoriented.

"Tell me, handsome. What's your name?"

I brought the microphone to my mouth. I heard a general laugh.

"André," I stuttered.

The audience cracked up again, like canned laughter in sitcoms. Then I realized that the microphone was a huge pink dildo. A very realistic one! I wanted to die.

"Ooh-la-la," Magnesia said. "And that accent? Where are you from?"

"French," I mumbled.

"Oh baby," Magnesia told Electra. "Tell him not to eat the microphone up; we need it for the show."

Earth, eat me whole! I looked where Lucy was sitting, hoping she'd come to my rescue, but when I found my bearings and located her in the shadows, I saw her bring her cell phone in front of her face and the glow of the flash. That little slut had taken my photo!

Since Lucy was not going to help me, I looked back at Tony. He was on a stool next to me, blindfolded, his hands tied behind his back, but unlike me he seemed to be enjoying the ride. He looked very sexy, with a lock of hair hanging down his face to one side of his nose and his mouth half open, hinting at the depth of his throat.

And then I dropped my dick. The plastic one, I mean. The mike.

I don't know how it happened, but it fell, and I couldn't think of anything else but crouching down to pick it up. I almost did, but it started rolling on the floor, don't ask me how, just when I practically had it. Finally, I pounced on it with both hands, and I ended up center stage on all fours, holding the dildo.

Then I felt some fingers in my kidneys and heard a new wave of canned laughter, yet another one, overlapping the first chords of Madonna's "Like a Virgin." I turned my head and found Magnesia glued to my butt, staring blankly at the ceiling, as if he were sodomizing me. I looked straight ahead again, only to see the pink penis between my eyes as an extension of my nose. Beyond, the pitch-dark amphitheater lit up for a second with camera flashes. My eyes filled with tears, and I felt like I was going to break down at any time. Luckily, in a moment of lucidity, I realized that there are times in life when we must play the whore's part and that it is simply better to accept it, so at the inner cry of Vive la différence! I got up with dignity, tore my shirt open, and tied it to my head like a veil. People egged me on shouting encouragement and whistling. I held the dildo as if it were a bouquet of flowers and walked like a virgin bride to where Tony was, to the rhythm of Madonna's song. Occasionally, I would give a thrust of the hip or stick my ass out, to the audience's delight. On my promenade, I improvised the choreography. First, I pushed a spiteful Magnesia out of the way. Then I jumped over Electra, who was crawling at my feet pleading for my love. And finally, I left Susie knocked out with a blow from the dildo. Poor Susie, being the least savvy, didn't know very well what to do with himself. By the time I sat on Tony's lap with my legs crossed over my thighs and grabbed him by the neck, the entire audience was standing and screaming. I took Tony's blindfold off, pushed the "veil" off my forehead in the Miss Piggy of Sesame Street style, and gave him a long kiss.

A star was born. Or maybe a slut, who knew.

And just think; I hadn't come to dance!

It was almost midnight when Lucy and I entered her apartment, panting after climbing five stories, and a little tipsy too. We had stopped at the landing on the fourth floor to straighten our spines against the wall and, while we were at it, we'd started laughing hard and being silly at the memory of my stellar show at Pink Velvet. The glow of the lights that were still on in the adjoining office building illuminated the living room, enveloping the few furniture pieces—a square Ikea dining table, three mismatched vintage chairs, and the sofa bed at the end—in the same silver glow of a full-moon night. Who would still be working so late?

I was surprised that Lucy didn't turn on the light, so I decided to do it myself, but before I could hit the switch, I felt her fingertips on my knuckles. Then she took my hand and placed it on the lower part of her back, as if it had always belonged there.

"My dreams are in black and white," she whispered as she got closer, finally resting her head on my chest and her hands on my torso.

"It's late," I said.

And it was. It was late for our story and late for me.

"Why? Are you going to turn into a pumpkin?" She unbuttoned my shirt's first button, stroked my Adam's apple, and made a ringlet with my newly unveiled chest hairs. Then she caressed the back of my neck, stirring up the dying embers of Tony's caress in the bathroom and the strange intimacy of our kiss onstage. I saw him again with his gelled hair, his perfect smile, and his eyes so deep blue you could barely tell the iris from the pupil.

"Lucy, I ..." I said in a whisper full of doubts.

She stood on tip toe. I felt her breasts crawling up my chest and then, without warning, her wet lips on mine. I opened my mouth for a quick frolic of our tongues, then turned my face away. I looked at her. She had her eyes closed, her head back, and the half-smile of someone still waiting to go on playing. I stroked her eyelids, followed with my fingers the contour of her ears, and kissed her like I'd kiss my sister. She made a face and stiffened as if I had a corpse in my arms. I turned on the light. All the details until then covered by darkness came to life: my suitcase next to the wall, the folded pajamas on the sofa, and, on the table, the dirty coffee cup with the open sugar bowl.

Lucy started to cry.

"I am silly," she said, drying her eyes with her sleeve. Then she laughed, in that absurd shame-hiding way that we have all laughed sometimes.

I held her face between my hands. I kissed her forehead.

"Get off me," she practically begged and pushed me away. She turned around, released her hair, waved it in the air, and quickly disappeared through the bathroom door.

I was left alone in that tiny living room that suddenly became huge. I had to explain to Lucy the reason behind my rejection of her. I sat on the sofa. There was nowhere else to go. Lucy was in the bathroom, and I wasn't going to get into her bedroom. I wasn't going to keep hiding either. Not anymore.

After a while, she came to sit beside me. Her face was washed, and her hair fastened behind her ears. She smiled.

"Sorry, my hormones are all over the place."

I remembered that the worst fights with Samantha used to coincide with the days before she had her period, so I already knew from experience that the less I spoke and the more neutral my comments the better.

"There's nothing to forgive," I said.

"You kissed me like you'd kiss your dog," she said, looking relaxed and calm.

I had to tell her. If I didn't tell her now, I would never tell her. Why did I find it so hard? What if she didn't look at me the same way? What if I lost her?

She got ahead of me. "There is a chance I've got cancer," she said, her eyes suddenly flooded.

I felt terrible again, not only because Lucy had cancer but because she'd been braver than me.

"Come here," I hugged her. She let herself get cozy in my arms.

Then she looked at me and coughed a laugh to fight the raising emotion. It was as if she were ashamed of her tears.

"Tony had insinuated something," I said as my small private revenge against him. "That's why I stopped all this. Do you want to talk?"

Lucy seemed relieved, and I concluded that the big problem with lies is that sometimes they work.

"Today I had some tests repeated, but I'd better start accepting the news."

"When will you know for sure?"

"In a couple of days."

Cancer. It sounded terrible, awful, but I was assuming the worst again. I remembered Lucy's words in the taxi about Tony. "When you get the short straw," she'd said. Now that phrase took on a new dimension. How could this happen to Lucy, to my Lucy? I didn't think it was the right time to ask what kind of cancer she had. I gave her a renewed long hug, and I didn't make it last longer so that she wouldn't think I felt sorry for her. I really didn't. The brave way she'd announced her illness had turned my friend into a goddess, and I just wanted to give her all the strength of my love. That's all I could think of while I held her in my arms. Courage, Lucy, courage. We told each other so much without saying one word!

Then her cell phone beeped with a text message.

"I love you," I whispered in her ear before separating my body from hers. She kissed me between neck and ear.

"It's from Tony," she said after checking her cell phone.

I gently ripped the phone from her hand and left it on the sofa's armrest.

"I also have to tell you something," I said, feeling a lump in my throat. In twenty seconds, I went through all twenty-two years of friendship like they say it happens just before you die. In a way, what I was about to tell her meant the death of the André she'd known all along. Everything I did or said from that moment on would be subject to a new interpretation.

In addition to my unfounded fear of rejection, I had another reason to bite my tongue. I was afraid Lucy would question the authenticity of our entire shared past. I didn't want her to think that our story had not been true.

And there was something else. Deep inside, I believed women, including Lucy, loved me only as long as they trusted—if only conceptually—in the possibility of a romance. This belief had devastating effects, as it implied I basically had no value without that flirty magic that floated in the air and to which I attributed the foundations of my relationships.

I finally told her:

"I'm not that different from Tony."

If it had cost me an arm to come out with Lucy, it had cost me a leg to use Tony as the paradigm of my sexual orientation. He represented everything I hated most about the gay scene and surely about myself. But it also seemed fair to recognize in some way that although Tony had toyed with me and even humiliated me in the Pink Velvet, he had also taught me an important lesson I needed to learn. I was no better than him.

Now I needed to convince myself that I wasn't any worse than anybody either, so while I waited for Lucy to respond, I looked in the bottom of her violet eyes for some clue as to how she would react to the news.

SATURDAY

When I woke up in the morning, it took me a while to get oriented. I was in Lucy's bed, but only the trace of her body on the mattress remained. As I got more alert, I remembered what had happened. I crept into the dining room. My pajamas were still folded on the couch, exactly as I had left them on the previous afternoon. Lucy was barefoot and fiddling with breakfast. She was wearing the same Yankees T-shirt to her knees she had slept in. Her hair was messy and loosely held by a plastic clip at the back of her neck.

"You snore," she said affectionately, and offered me coffee and a bagel with cream cheese.

We sat at the table for breakfast.

Lucy and I had slept in the same bed, not for sex, or just for love. We had spent the night embracing each other in a sort of light sleep because we were both scared. Our common denominator had been fear.

Because of fear, she hadn't told me about her cancer when I'd called her to announce my trip to New York. Because of fear, she didn't tell me at the airport, or later at home when we were chatting before she went to get her the tests redone and I took my nap. Out of fear, and not for lack of opportunity, she avoided telling me in the taxi, where instead she'd found the time to clue me in on Tony's HIV status. And out of fear she'd kissed me in what she thought was her last chance of being seen as the same old Lucy.

"I was afraid you'd love me less," she'd summed up, hugging the pillow.

My very same fear.

"And you, silly," she told me at breakfast, "did you think I would love you more if I got laid?"

I shrugged.

"Really?" she exclaimed and left the cup on her plate.

She then took my hand and told me exactly what I needed to hear:

"I love you because you are sensitive and affectionate."

I smiled, appeased.

"And because you make me laugh. Yesterday in the Pink you surpassed yourself."

"Go on, keep on ..." I so needed to hear that!

"Want to know something else?"

I nodded, although I almost preferred to leave things as they stood.

"You were better as a friend than as a lover," she said so sweetly that, far from bothering me, her comment made me love her more.

"Who else knows?" she asked me after a few seconds of reflection.

I said nothing.

"Samantha?"

"But she doesn't quite believe it. The other day she asked me if I wanted to have more children. We haven't talked about it again."

"Christine?"

"Are you crazy?"

"You will have to tell her"

"We'll see. Right now, I can't see the need. Maybe the day I meet somebody."

"And who have you been venting with?"

I told her about my confidants Bernadette and François, but I omitted that he had been the first man I'd had full on sex with. For a long time, the only one. The rest had just been flirtations. I didn't feel like going back in time and rewriting all my divorce book. All that was over and done with.

"It must have been hard," she concluded.

"Let's talk about something else, could we?" I didn't want her to feel sorry for me. "What I'd really like to know is how I can help you."

She replied she would love to go with me see John. That day had arrived.

"It's just that it seems such an amazing story," she said.

I promised her she'd be my confidant, my Watson, my everything, but I wanted to go by myself. I only had an address, so I had no choice but to show up at his place and trust that, when the time was right, I had enough courage to knock on his door and introduce myself.

"I don't know how I would take it if a stranger stood at my door with such a tale," she warned me. "On top of that, you are a foreigner. You can't even imagine the problem you would have if you were black."

"It's not a tale. It's a true story."

But she was right. I didn't have a clue about how John would react when I told him about an unknown mother and brother.

"That's why I don't want you to come. It's too risky," I added.

That was just half true because in a way I wanted to be the only one to pay this last tribute to Michele. As if she cared. She was dead.

"Just be careful, do you promise? Here people have weapons."

I sighed. She talked like my mother.

"And they use them," she added very circumspectly. "I'm telling you. In this country they shoot first and then they ask questions."

I dressed hurriedly. I wanted to get started with my day. When I was about to leave, Lucy came to wish me luck.

"Before I forget," she said, "do you remember Tony's message? Last night's ..."

I did. It had precipitated my coming out to her. Actually, Tony had done me a favor. I much preferred telling her directly rather than having Tony lay it out for me. But now that I'd put my cards on the table, I was curious to know how he would have described to Lucy the grope below the tablecloth, our duel in the bathroom, and especially what he'd felt when I kissed him onstage.

"He wanted your phone number. Should I give it to him?"

I remembered what Tony had told me right after the drag queens had freed us, and we were walking back to our table:

"We don't have to leave this at just a kiss."

"Leave what? Wasn't this just a game?" I'd answered.

As it turned out, he hadn't shared any juicy details with her, none of the backstage action, so she had seen the same cheeky and fun performance as the rest of the audience. The remainder of the evening had passed uneventfully except for a couple of times Tony and I had—quite invitingly—sized each other up. The farewell had been cold. I was dead tired.

My face turned pink at the memory of the give and take with Tony. It was scary that I didn't know what I was capable of doing. The darkness had provided me with the excuse to unleash my instincts. Surely being in New York had something to do with it, perhaps the jetlag, and certainly the gin & tonic—I told myself—but in the daylight, desire died off quickly, and the events of last evening seemed to me now more a dream than an actuality. And like dreams, which can be vividly remembered right after waking up and then either forgotten or transformed, Tony now appeared blurry. Likely, lust would return the minute it got dark again, but right then it was 9:30 on a sunny early May Saturday, and I had a mission to fulfill.

"Then what, should I give him your number or not?" Lucy insisted.

"Why do you think he wants it?" I said as I combed my hair in front of a very 70's sun-shaped brass mirror which hung next to the entrance. I wanted to find out if that was all Tony had said in his message.

Lucy didn't answer me.

"Let's do something," I said. "I'll leave it up to you. If you think that's best for me ... Now I have to go," I concluded and blew her a kiss.

"Please be careful," I heard her shout before the door closed behind me.

While I was going down the stairs, I regretted not having taken hold of my own destiny. Tony had asked for my number, and the answer to that was either "yes" or "no." That was the mature way of making decisions. Did I want to sleep with Tony, yes or no? In the end, it all came down to that. I started to walk down the street. I would talk to Lucy when I came back home later that afternoon and give her my answer. I had the whole day to think about which one.

I took the subway to Penn Station and then managed to get on the 10:24 train to Chatham only because it was a little late leaving. It was a small miracle to find myself on the right train and to find an empty seat, with no one sitting next to me. Lucky for me, it was Saturday. According to Google maps, from the Chatham train station it was a ten-minute walk to John's house at 4 Oak Terrace. John Patten, that's what he was called after adoption. What name would Michele have given him? She never told me. Michele and I didn't have much time for conversation on that final phone call in Barcelona, the last time we met.

I had searched "John Patten" on the internet, but none were listed in Chatham. I wanted to call him before showing up. While going through the tunnel under New York City I thought about how hard it must have been for Michele to live through nine months of pregnancy, suffer the pain of childbirth, see his face, wait for him to cry, touch him and probably also kiss him, count his fingers and toes, and then say goodbye. How does one survive knowing that a part of you lives somewhere else, and that he lives without you and practically despite you? I could not imagine life without Christine. What would she be doing now?

I hadn't realized how deep into Spring we were until the train rode away from Manhattan and we came out of the tunnels. The leafy treetops were a pleasant surprise as there weren't many trees in the city, except in Central Park. In the suburbs, the trees lined up along the sidewalks and around the stations' parking lots. Some peeked between office buildings or stood in the sparse empty lots. The only thing those trees had in common was that someone had planted all of them. A few minutes later, the imposing profile of the skyscrapers began to look like a cutout held up to the horizon. The trees became more frequent and taller the smaller and more scattered the buildings were. Soon, it was the single-family homes with their porches and their gardens that had been built into the thick of the forest and not the other way around. I tried to identify the species, but I am not exactly an expert in botany. I knew some things about oak and cherry trees because their wood is used for barrels, and, although American oak is different from French, at the end of the day it's still oak. I also recognized the willows because we had those at home. We passed through a grove of white pines and in the distance, I spotted a couple of majestic firs. They were not nearly as tall as those of Ribeauvillé, one of which is the tallest in France. At least in the tall fir category we beat the Americans.

When the train stopped at my station, it was almost 11:45. I thought I should have gotten up earlier or left sooner because I was going to turn up at John's house at lunchtime, and it seemed inappropriate. Maybe he had family, and I'd interrupt their lunch, but then I remembered what Michele had mentioned in her letter about John being "alone in the world." Wasn't I just there to ease his loneliness with the news about Dawson? Wasn't that my mission?

Ultimately, I hadn't undertaken the trip only for Michele. I wasn't as good a person as Lucy had described me. The idea of helping John was somehow redemptive. I'd known the bitterness of feeling lonely as I had felt with Samantha in the last months of our marriage. That was the worst kind of loneliness, the one you feel when you live with someone who doesn't love you anymore.

Oak Terrace was a pretty cul-de-sac ending in a small maple forest, with four wooden two-story houses on each side, all either gray, white or blue. The American flag waved in front of each of them and on the last one, in addition, the flag of Cuba or Puerto Rico. I always got them confused. John's house was painted an off white. It was the first house on the left at the corner of another slightly wider street, Chestnut Avenue, which in turn was a branch of the road coming from the train station. His lawn was perfectly trimmed shining in the Spring sun as if it had just been watered.

Six steps lined with lilac and white petunia terracotta pots climbed up to the porch. From the ceiling hung some ferns symmetrically arranged over a pair of rocking chairs. The door, wedged between two windows, was London phone booth red. Above the peephole you could read "Patten" in white and lilac ceramic letters, like the petunias. To the left, between the door and the window, an iron salamander was stuck on the wall watching a matching fly placed on the other side. Everything was arranged so orderly and tastefully that it struck me that a woman lived in that house.

I crossed Chestnut Avenue to expand my view of the house. I needed to get some distance to look at the entire picture. I wanted to find some masculinity in the whole, since there definitely wasn't any in some of the parts. But even from further away, John's house looked somewhat feminine, with curtains on the windows and a flowering hedge that ran around the garden.

Suddenly, it hit me that I may be drawing too much attention in that residential neighborhood. If it wasn't for the SUV's parked in the driveways no one seemed to live here. There wasn't a single living soul on the street. I stood by an old bus stop and thought, "And now what?"

I was weighing whether to knock on his door or leave and whether it was fair to disturb John's life or reprehensible to be shaking up his past, when a man who'd just been jogging passed by my side. He wore a gray sweatshirt, his back wet with fresh sweat and his head covered by a hood. He was holding a paper bag from Dunkin' Donuts and was accompanied by two white Argentine bulldogs, strong like wolves with their mouths oozing foam, and looking at me with menacing eyes. He went by me so quickly that I didn't have a chance to see his face. He didn't pay any attention to me either, distracted as he was with the dogs. It didn't even occur to me that it could be John. I thought he was going to keep walking straight, but then he crossed the street and in the blink of an eye climbed the porch steps, pushed open the door, and entered his house followed by his two beasts. I'd barely had time to think that, whoever he was, he had a nice ass and a well-built body. "So John is hot."

Then I heard a voice. It came from the house opposite John's. In the window overlooking Chestnut Avenue, a stocky, bald man in his mid-fifties, dressed in a red and black plaid lumberjack shirt, spotted me.

"Can I help you with something?" he shouted, his voice as unfriendly as the expression on his face.

He had not given me the chance to respond when he added:

"The bus doesn't stop there anymore. Now it goes down Lexington. Are you sure I can't help you with anything?"

I shoved my hands in my pockets and shook my head.

"Then get out of here, or I'll call the police," he said and brusquely closed the window like a guillotine.

That evening, Lucy and I went out to dinner at a Thai restaurant on the corner of 120th street. I had no choice but to face the music.

"What do you mean, you only saw his ass?" she asked in disbelief when I summed up the scene. "Don't tell me you went all the way to fricking Chatham to only see his ass!" she chastised me with a mixture of English and French and then took a sip of her beer. She grabbed the bottle by the base, not by the neck as Samantha did.

"And how is it that you just turned around and left?" she added while deftly hooking the noodles of the pad Thai on the chopsticks. She seemed a bit disappointed. She hadn't asked a question but had made an accusation that led to an interrogation. I said, no, I had not knocked on his door. Yes, John was alone—well, with his bulldogs. Again, no, he had not seen me, but the neighbor did. And I told her how I had rushed away after his threats from the window.

"I am telling you, that guy doesn't live by himself, Lucy," I said.

I described the refinement, the neatness, and the two matching rocking chairs. That—she'd have to admit—was irrefutable.

"I live alone, and I have three chairs."

I tried to make Lucy understand that it was not only difficult but also terribly awkward to show up at John's. It wasn't like I was used to going from door to door selling encyclopedias. "Encyclopedias, God, that's how old I am." I really hoped for John to have a wife or at least a girlfriend. Then he wouldn't be alone as Michele had said, and I'd lose any legitimacy to invade his life in such an abrupt way while keeping my dignity intact.

"You looked at the mailbox, right?" Lucy inquired.

"The mailbox," I repeated.

She looked at me as if I were dumb.

"Tomorrow I am going with you," she asserted.

Fortunately, Lucy couldn't come with me the next day because she worked, but she threatened to ask for Monday off if I didn't promise to try again.

"You can't make this trip for nothing," she rightly said.

"By the way," I said, changing the subject, "in the end, please don't give Tony my number."

Lucy set the chopsticks on the table.

"You're going to kill me. Since you left it up to me ... May I ask you why?"

I hated to be forced to admit the reasons because I realized how flimsy they were. Ultimately, it was always fear. Michele had already hit the nail on the head on the first day, when she'd asked me at the entrance of Fort Schoenenbourg what my Maginot Line was. What a divine way to ask what I was afraid of.

Oddly enough, this time I had carefully studied the reasons why I didn't want to meet Tony again. I had thought it over and over on the train on the way back from Chatham, and, although I went back and forth a few times throughout the journey, by the time I reached Penn Station I'd made up my mind.

"I don't want to sleep with my demons," I said, proud to have been able to condense all my wisdom in one sentence.

I went back to my green curry chicken. I hated chopsticks. A fork would work better.

"You mean with your neurosis?" she wondered.

I looked up. It was like having dinner with Woody Allen himself.

In all honesty, I didn't feel like talking about this with Lucy. That night I wanted to chat about rice noodles and soy sauce, the best way to pick up your chopsticks, or why Asians cover their mouths when they laugh. I wanted to complain about the price of beer and understand why we had to leave a twenty percent tip. If she wanted to, we could go into how she was going to face her illness and the ways I could help her cope. There was still room for hope. Her diagnosis wasn't confirmed yet. We would know more in a week, when she got the results of the new tests back. We had to stay optimistic. Keeping on harping on my obsessions, no thanks. The weekend had already been hectic enough.

"I'm sorry, you know we therapists," she said.

Lucy was not a psychologist, but she worked in an emotional therapy center. She'd told me what it was that she did, but the truth is that I hadn't quite understood it. Something similar to reiki.

"If he calls you, don't answer and that's it," she said, returning to the topic of Tony.

We left the restaurant early. Lucy went to bed as soon as we got home, and I stayed up a little longer. There were no kisses that night, or hugs or, for that matter, any other shows of affection, fear, or lust. We just wished each other good night, which ordinarily wouldn't have been enough, but was just wonderful after the excess of the day before. I had trouble falling asleep because I was invaded by feelings of dread. While trying to make myself comfortable for Morpheus—would he be gay as well?—I questioned my attitude these days. Was I living up to Lucy's expectations? Maybe I was grasping at straws by betting it all on the hope card. She probably didn't want to be constantly reminded that Damocles' sword was hanging over her, but perhaps I was ignoring the problem too much. I was not prepared. We are not educated to deal with this type of situation. I knew that if my worst fears were confirmed, I'd live up to what was expected of me, but the time had already come to do something special for Lucy. But what? I didn't want to go too far or fall short. And there was also Tony. If I liked him, why didn't I sleep with him? Things were quite the opposite from what I'd told Lucy. If I didn't have sex with Tony, that's when my demons would win. But how was I going to have sex with someone who had AIDS? It was unthinkable that I was considering it. To top it off, there was also Michele's shadow. I was still chewing on whether to meet John.

Suddenly, I needed air, so I sat up. I felt observed and a little dizzy when I stood up to investigate. I waved the curtains back and forth to make sure there was no one hidden behind them. How ridiculous of me. I finally figured out what I was feeling. It was anxiety. That explained why I felt stifled and couldn't breathe. I sat in one of the three chairs. A dim light sneaked under Lucy's door. She was still awake. What would she be thinking?

I would ask her tomorrow.

SUNDAY

Morpheus is not gay. Or, if he is, he didn't want to have sex with me that night.

On Sunday, I woke up full of energy and in a great, optimistic mood. Once I'd managed to fall asleep, I slept like a log. Blame it on fatigue and the compounded emotions built up during the previous two days—in fact, since I'd received Michele's letter. I decided to take advantage of my mood and left the apartment early, in case my mood changed later on. I had a shower and a glass of orange juice with some cookies before Lucy got up, the towel still wrapped around my waist. Lucy deserved a better breakfast than that, so I fixed her a zucchini omelet. I would have eaten a piece myself, but it was nicer looking without a triangle missing, so I held back. I topped it with two olives to make the eyes and drew a smile with a few almonds, just as I did when Christine was a little kid. Then I tidied up the best I could so as not to leave Lucy a mess, got dressed, and sped off. On my way to the subway, I got a bagel and a coffee to go. I wasn't in a hurry, but I was infected by the frantic New York pace. If John had the habit of jogging, he'd follow a routine, so I planned to get to Chatham about 11:30, like the day before.

Coming from Chestnut Avenue, Oak Terrace looked just as deserted as Saturday. I leaned back on the same old bus stop sign. John's house also appeared quiet. The lights on the first floor were off, and there was no sign of life on the second floor either. The only noticeable difference from the day before was the waving flag. The wind had picked up, and you could see the bars and the stars now. I scanned the other houses on the road, especially the corner one across the street from John's, and I sighed in relief at the drawn curtains on the side window where the angry man had stood the day before. Lucy was so right when warning me that the locals didn't beat around the bush. To go unnoticed, I had put on a baseball cap, but on the first day she had objected that I'd need to rethink my entire wardrobe, especially the pants, because no American of my age wore them so tight. With or without a cap, the truth is that anyone would stand out in such an off the beaten path neighborhood.

"Stop procrastinating," I told myself. There was absolutely no point in delaying the meeting any further. I crossed Chestnut Avenue, passed by Mister Nice's house, and took my first steps onto Oak Terrace. I stopped in front of John's house, my stomach rumbling. I felt like a child facing a haunted house. There were the salamander, the fly, and the red door. At times, they all seemed to come alive.

I made it to the bottom of the steps, where the mailbox was. "I knew it!" A plate attached to the mailbox said, "John and Martha Patten." So there was a Mrs. Patten, and her name was Martha. I wish Lucy had been there. I would have asked her to read it aloud to my delight. Surprisingly, Michele didn't know anything about this Martha. She didn't usually miss things, and it wasn't her style to trick me. The mailbox was closed, but a couple of letters and some grocery store brochures showed through the slot. I just had to look at one of the envelopes and hopefully get some clues on the Pattens. Then I'd put it back. That's it, end of story.

Was I crazy or what? How was I going to do such a thing? I looked to the right. At the end of the street, where the maple forest began, a kid's bicycle lay in the center of the road. I looked to the left. No one. I grabbed one of the letters by the corner and pulled, but it tore, and I was left with a little paper triangle between my fingers. I tried again. Eureka! I looked at the sender: Bank of America. It would probably be a statement. I felt the envelope. It contained a credit card. Then I heard a squeak behind me. I turned around in time to see the door of the crazy neighbor's house closing. I pictured the neighbor forcing the closet open and picking up a shotgun. While I was trying to decide which way to start running, John appeared at his door. He looked so different from Michele and the way I'd imagined him looking. Shit! How was I going to justify that I had his credit card in my hand? I didn't have much time to think about it before.

I heard a disturbing mixture of gasps and barks coming from inside the house, accompanied by the sound of claws slipping on a wooden floor. Before I knew it, John's two dogs had leapt on me from the top of the stairs, and I'd been thrown to the ground. I laid in the fetal position, my face down to keep it away from their jaws. The dogs kept pulling my clothes, until I felt a sharp and deep pain in my thigh, as if I had been stabbed with scissors.

"I know your mother," I shouted desperately.

I couldn't think of anything else to say, and it worked. Suddenly, the dogs gave up on their attack and moved some three feet away, constantly barking. I stood up, stunned and scared. My thigh ached, and I couldn't put weight on it. The animals were all excited, jumping around me and tracing semicircles in the air, their faces blue with anger.

John came down and calmed them. He looked at me suspiciously and asked me to excuse Hansel and Gretel, but I was convinced that they'd just obeyed his orders. "Hansel and Gretel? Poor little things," I thought. "Bastards!"

Soon the neighbor—named Hugo—joined us, his face inflamed and his fists clenched. John made a gesture with his hands that I interpreted as "Calm down, I'll take care of it." Then he stroked the slimy mouth of the bulldogs and tore the letter from my hands.

"So," John said straight to the point. "What did you know about my mother?"

"Exactly," Hugo growled, "how in hell did you know Martha?"

Hugo will never know, but he provided me with a lightbulb moment. John's adoptive mother was Martha. I remembered the inscription on the mailbox: "John and Martha Patten," and it took on a totally different meaning now. Everything fit together. John and Martha were John's parents, and this was their house. John and his father shared the same first name, which explained the mistake of having attributed a wife to John. A bark interrupted my thoughts. The bulldogs were so close that I could smell them, and their saliva dripped on my feet. I couldn't waste my time unraveling the Patten family tree. I had to come up with a satisfactory answer urgently.

"I'd rather not start with that," I said to buy time.

Hugo took a step forward. One of the dogs stood on its hind legs.

"You are not in a position to choose," Hugo said.

"I've come from France on a rather personal matter." I emphasized "from France." I shook off the gravel and the dried grass from my pants. I wanted to recover as neat an appearance as possible. The dogs sniffed my shoes and barked louder. They wanted me.

"A *private* matter," I said gazing at John in a desperate attempt to divide their alliance.

"I'm going to call the police," Hugo threatened. "We've heard enough bullshit."

John reached down and looked at my thigh, where the dogs had bitten me. He lifted the fabric. I'd suffered an L-shaped tear in my pants.

"This doesn't look good," he said far more sweetly than I expected given the circumstances. "Where did you say you are from?"

"Strasbourg."

They looked at each other, puzzled. Clearly, they had no idea where Strasbourg was.

"East of Paris. I arrived the day before yesterday," I said, quickly.

My heart was beating fast, and I was shaking. I still hadn't recovered from the dogs' behavior when Hugo snorted:

"We saved your ass, you know?"

"Who is we?" I thought. I didn't know what the madman was talking about.

"You'd be eating sauerkraut now," he added and spit on the ground.

"My name is André," I said, although no one had asked me. I hoped it would be harder to break the nose of someone whose name you knew.

"André, you are full of shit," Hugo said, his face deep red. The calmer I tried to behave, the more enraged he acted.

"I can apply some hydrogen peroxide and iodine on this if you let me," said John.

He had an uncommon yet, for some reason, familiar face. None of his features, taken separately, could be described as beautiful, but the whole was harmonious. He was one of those attractively unremarkable but very masculine looking guys. I looked at him more closely. I still couldn't find any resemblance to Michele. Maybe his lips were thin like hers?

"Are you fucking with me, John?" Hugo protested. "This guy has been prowling around the street the entire weekend; he's stolen your mail; and now you are going to invite him into your house to put a band aid on him?"

"What I have to tell you is important," I said, seeing a glimmer of hope, "and quite private," I insisted, challenging Hugo. "We can go to a coffee place, if you'd like."

John left me alone with the dogs and took Hugo a few feet away. I don't know what he told him, but after a brief conversation the two men hugged. John tapped Hugo on the back, and Hugo went back to his house. Before closing the door, he turned around and brought two of his fingers to his eyes as a warning that he'd be watching me. It was a ridiculous and childish gesture, but I was glad to see him go.

"You'd be the first Frenchman in history to cross the Atlantic just to steal mail in Chatham," John said. He gestured to the dogs to stay out and invited me in. It was dark inside and smelled of the same fresh and clean cologne he used.

"Do you live alone?" I asked as soon as the door closed behind us. I immediately regretted being foolhardy.

"Come in," he said ignoring my question. He led me into the living room, which was at the end of the hall past the stairs that led up to the second floor, and motioned to the sofa. "I'll go get the first aid kit."

John turned around and disappeared. I heard the stairs creaking and then his steps on the ceiling over my head. The beams were old, and the wooden floors complained. In the living room there were two identical green velvet armchairs separated by a small table containing a telephone, a notebook, and a plastic pen. I sat in the chair which was closest to the hall. I was tempted to steal the pen. In hotels I always took them as souvenirs. The blinds at the back of the room were closed, but some light filtered between the strips and reflected on a walnut table surrounded by four chairs. When I turned on the lamp next to me, the reliefs of acanthus leaves on the alabaster fireplace came alive. The bronze clock that rested on the mantelpiece said 11.50. I was surprised by the classic interior, but I quickly realized that the decoration was leftover from John's parents.

However, the most intriguing part was at the opposite end of the room. It appeared to be an annex with tile flooring instead of parquet and a rougher texture on the walls. It was an artist studio. Against the wall, under the three large windows, I saw a metal table covered by an oilcloth, on top of which were an abundance of glass jars and colored pots, a roll of paper towels, and two jugs with brushes of various lengths and thicknesses. On the corner of the table there was a lamp with a square shade. Next to the back wall, where the windows ended, an easel rested on a large acrylic sheet. On the easel was a half-painted picture of a human figure. Behind, on the floor, three unframed canvases rested one behind the other. The one in the foreground was brightly colored. To the right of the easel there was a bench long enough to accommodate three people covered with books and magazines. I assumed they were art related, although from this distance I couldn't see them in detail. It was clear that John, at least in his spare time, enjoyed painting. He was an artist.

"Focus," I told myself. I didn't have much time to think about how I was going to start the conversation. Did John know he was adopted? I still doubted whether I should tell him or not, but at this point there was no turning back. After my unfortunate introduction, my best choice was to be honest, settle this issue as soon and gracefully as possible, and continue with my life. I needed to return to Manhattan, walk through Central Park, and visit the Metropolitan Museum. It was time for me to stop playing detective and behave like any other tourist in New York.

It didn't take John long to come back down. He carried a little box.

"Maybe one day I can make a living painting. For the time being, I'm just a sad accountant," he said when he realized I was curiously looking toward his studio.

He sat, his knees open, on a maroon and black carpet like the ones I'd seen in Marrakech. He looked like Aladdin.

"I would ask you to undress but we are not quite there yet," he joked and lifted the scissors. "I am afraid I'll have to cut your pants. They are ruined anyway."

He began to trim around the rip. He had traces of paint on his hands.

"You don't know my mother at all, right?" he said as if nothing had happened.

I was a little disturbed by the triviality with which he spoke of something so important.

"If the question is 'do I know Martha?' the answer is no, I don't."

I felt the cold steel of the scissors brushing my skin.

"Martha and John died last year. Are your parents alive?" he said as he completed cutting a circle on the cloth.

"No, but I have a daughter. Why do you call your parents by their first name?"

"It's a long story. I would like to have a child one day."

He applied alcohol to a cotton ball like the ones Samantha used to remove her makeup.

"I suspect that your story has something to do with what I've come to tell you. Does the name Michele ring a bell at all?" I looked into his eyes. They were brown, a little close together, with long, thick, and curly eyelashes. They showed serenity and nobility.

"Does it hurt?" he said, while he pressed the cotton against the bite.

"No, but it stings."

"It's normal. The wound is fresh."

John stopped pressing on the wound. He tapped it a couple of times and blew on it, causing me to experience a combination of burn and tickle. I wasn't expecting that, but I liked it. If he did this to me, what wouldn't he do for someone he loved?

"Michele Keller. Do you know her?" I insisted.

He picked up another cotton ball, dipped it in alcohol, and pressed harder on my wound. He stared at me. He was trying to hide that I'd hit a nerve.

"I didn't know her last name."

I was relieved and surprised that he knew of Michele's existence. Would he know anything about Dawson?

"She told me about you. Michele asked me to come."

John put the scissors, the alcohol, and the cotton back into the first aid kit.

"I don't have iodine," he said, lying. I'd seen the yellow bottle between some gauze.

He got up and walked to the last window before the painting studio. That annex was probably his sanctuary. He opened the blinds. A large beam of light illuminated the room, revealing John's athletic silhouette against the glass. I couldn't see his face, just his back.

"Now you are going to tell me that she has died too," he said after a while.

I kept quiet. John remained impassive looking toward the garden.

"I'm going to give you my number," I said and wrote it down on the pad on the table. It was from a hotel called P-Town Dreams. "Call me if you want to know more."

I made a move to get up, but I felt a strong pain in the thigh. John turned around, removed his hair from his eyes, and crossing his arms asked me:

"What was she like?"

The image of a rose like those in Turkey Michele had spoken to me about once came to my mind.

"Complicated, why say otherwise."

John looked puzzled, as if he'd expected a different answer.

"Ladies often are," I added. I said it without hesitation, even if it sounded dated, because I was convinced that word defined Michele better than any other. She was, above all, a lady.

"What was she to you?" he asked, pressing me further. I wasn't prepared to answer that question. Instead of saying "a friend," I started to chew on what she'd really meant to me.

A mother? No, despite the age difference, our feelings had not been of that kind. Ten percent, I decided on a quick calculation, as if I could put a percentage on what one feels. A lover? Neither! The idea had seemed to me once both appealing and disgusting and had had a lot to do with the decision not to see her anymore. But no, how could we possibly be lovers? Travel companion? We had seen half the world together, but I wouldn't consider her just that, and to be fair, she wasn't a traditional friend either, like Lucy or Bernadette. I remembered something she had told me several times: "Please, don't give us a label."

I could not do it.

"She loved me unconditionally," I replied when John was already starting to get impatient. "That kind of love is very difficult to come by."

"What have you come for?" John said sharply. He had his hands on his waist now, his chest out, and he looked at me haughtily. I was taken aback by this turnaround. His reaction was that of someone who'd already made up his mind about Michele a long time ago and was disturbed at the mere idea of changing it. I guess he couldn't possibly agree with what I'd just told him. A lady who loves without conditions would not have abandoned him.

"Your mother asked me to. I already told you that."

I was going in circles, and that wasn't good. I had to tell him about Dawson and couldn't come up with a way.

"That woman is not my mother," he said with determination. "My mother's name was Martha, and as I said she died last year."

I summoned my courage and asked him how he'd heard the name of Michele before.

"Children are neither deaf nor dumb. In this house there were always four of us."

I wasn't surprised at his statement. Once Michele broke into your life, it was to stay.

"Do you think you can walk?" he asked me. "Do you want me to call a taxi?"

He was throwing me out—very politely—and I still hadn't transmitted my message. My pulse accelerated.

"You have a brother," I said bluntly.

John let out a short laugh.

"I'll call you a taxi. Do you have Uber?"

Why was he being defensive?

"His name is Dawson, and he lives here, well, in New York," I said hastily.

"You know what? Call it yourself," he said.

He then took me by the arm, helped me get up, and walked me to the door. I couldn't go as fast as he wished because my leg hurt when I walked. I was limping. When we arrived at the door, he said:

"You can wait for it out there. Sit in one of the rocking chairs if you want."

Then he slammed the door in my face.

I found myself on the street again, bruised, my pants torn, limping, and feeling as ashamed and humiliated as on the Pink Velvet stage, where I had barely contained my tears. I sensed that in the apparent solitude of Oak Terrace there was, as in the Pink, an audience hidden in the shadows. Behind me, John would be standing by the window, and surely Hugo was also watching me, ready to call the police at the slightest opportunity or to shoot me, who knows. As I went down the steps, I realized that I could stand the pain, so I decided to walk back to the train station. When I reached the bottom of the stairs, the damn dogs appeared from behind the house. They didn't touch me this time. Instead, they took pity on me and escorted me to the corner with Chestnut Avenue where they just stopped, as if they'd run into an electrified fence.

On the way to the station, I felt more optimistic. Maybe things hadn't gone so badly after all. I had complied with Michele's instructions and felt liberated. Now John knew that he had a brother, and the ball lay in his court. He had behaved politely. He had invited me into his house after catching me red-handed stealing his mail and had even dressed my wound. He had stoically endured the news I'd given him, which was not easy to digest, and had blown on my wound, as if I were a child who'd just fallen off his bicycle. That had really been an unexpected sign of attentiveness. I always care about these small details. They're important to me, even though I am not always thoughtful myself. How would I have reacted? Not half as well.

As for Hugo, I'd better forget about him. He had done nothing but protect his friend and maybe try to settle who knows what outstanding historical debt between the United States and France.

As I watched the train approach the station, I was glad that John, Hugo, and my debt to Michele were about to be left behind in that pretty town in New Jersey. Soon I'd be back in the lights of Manhattan. I'd visit the Metropolitan and the Guggenheim but first a small museum called the Frick that Lucy had told me not to miss. I'd go that afternoon, as soon as I arrived in New York City. I also wanted to go to the theater before returning to France but not the Pink Velvet! I'd go watch a musical, at least one. *The Book of Mormon* had been recommended to me. I was sure that Lucy would love to come with me, as it would keep her distracted for a few hours.

I got on the train car. I looked out the window. Bye-bye, Chatham. Sayonara, I thought without any nostalgia as I put my head back and got ready to rest. Shortly, the landscape would run behind the window, the gray cement quickly replacing the green trees, and in an hour I'd be joining the other ants in the big city. My plan was delayed. Time went by, and the train didn't move. Apparently, there had been an accident—we were told later that someone had been hit—and we'd be stopped at the station until further notice.

Trapped in Chatham. Was it an omen?

As Lucy had told me, the Frick Museum was a real gem next to Central Park, and it was open on Sunday afternoons. I was a little afraid when I got there that they wouldn't let me in in my torn pants and looking as if I'd just fought in Afghanistan, but I was forgetting that we were in New York. Once I washed my face and combed my hair with water at a nearby Mc Donald's, I looked much better, and nobody at the box office or at the entrance even looked at me. As advertised, the museum had once been the palace of steel magnate Henry Clay Frick, who made arrangements for the building and the art collection to be open to visitors after he and his wife died. The minute I went in, before even touring the neoclassical rooms arranged around the sublime courtyard, I knew that I would find in this place exactly what I needed: peace and beauty. I turned off my cell phone. I wanted to be alone and breathe in the smell of the aged tulle curtains and centuries-old oils, take a break from that crazy weekend, and reflect on what I expected from life. Yes, this was the perfect place to philosophize for a couple of hours on the search for happiness and the essence of myself.

The collection was eclectic but wonderful, arranged as if the Fricks still lived there. I stopped, despite not being a religious person, in front of a fourteenth century painting depicting Christ carrying the cross on his back. I thought that life sometimes weighed on us as much as that huge cross on the golden background weighed on Christ. In another room, I was moved by a chiaroscuro showing a mother with her baby in her arms. There was something tragic about it. While the woman's features were clearly distinguishable, the baby's figure was a blur. Could he be dead? I looked more closely. She was breastfeeding him. What was the painter intending to express? I looked at who had painted it. *Maternity*, by Eugène Carrière. French, nineteenth century. I didn't know him. I couldn't help but think again what it would have meant for Michele to give up John for adoption, but right away I tried to get the idea out of my mind. It was turning into a recurring thought. I went on walking. I felt good in this place, each room with a fireplace and leather armchairs, and the furniture and objects Mr. Frick had been collecting throughout his life: Chinese vases, bronze statues, crystal chandeliers. I walked slowly, one would think randomly, stopping here and there. But it was no coincidence that I practically dodged a Velázquez and yet almost cried when facing two cloud sketches by Constable. When I looked at them, I remembered Michele's words on the day we'd met: "Constable couldn't have painted a more beautiful sky," she'd said and then written again in her letter. And to think that, until then, I didn't even know who he was! There they were now, not one but two of his exquisite skies brimming with clouds. There had to be a day when Michele also saw them for the first time in this or another museum.

I went on walking. *Cupid Sacrificing His Wings for the Delight of the First Kiss*. The title of this little drawing on paper made me chuckle, and I went from laughter to nostalgia at the memories of the kiss with Tony at the Pink Velvet.

At the end of the tour there was a Pieta. Christ dead. It was 4:45 and the museum was about to close.

When I walked out onto the street it was March cold and threatening rain. There wasn't a bit of blue showing between the clouds, unlike in Constable's paintings. The sky was so dark that it engulfed the tallest skyscrapers. A wind carried a slight stench of docks and diesel from the distant Hudson River. I hailed a taxi and gave the driver Lucy's address. As soon as I sat down, my leg hurt again. I turned on my cell phone. I barely had any battery left. I had two text messages. One was from Christine, telling me that she loved me and to get her some Nikes. The other text from a local number said:

"Would you accept an apology? A drink and snacks?"

So Tony admitted that he hadn't treated me fairly. I thought he'd be prouder, but, as they say, a wise man changes his mind; a fool never.

"Today I can't. Tomorrow?" I wrote as an answer. I was worn out and that evening I just wanted to rest. I received his reply instantly:

"7:00 pm at the Rainbow Café" and an address.

I wasn't in the mood for another gay joint, but I ended up typing, "Ok, see you tomorrow" just as the screen lit up with a call from Lucy. She told me not to wait for her for dinner. That night I'd be on my own.

When I got to Lucy's place, I made myself some tea and sat down to watch old episodes of *I love Lucy*. How appropriate! During the commercial, I called Christine to see what model of sneakers she wanted and to get her size. At about 7:30 I went shopping. It was getting late, and many shops were shutting down. The road was wet after a shower. I went into a Foot Locker to get Christine shoes. Then I bought a blue cup with a yellow taxi on it and a gray sweatshirt from Columbia University with the university logo: a crown with three crosses. I paid five more dollars for a slice of pepperoni pizza and a coke at the corner restaurant and went back to the apartment. I showered and sat down to read *Madame Bovary*. I liked it. I had bought it at the airport. Nothing like a good classic.

I was sound asleep by 10:00 pm.

MONDAY

On Monday, I decided to surprise Lucy with a good breakfast, so I left the apartment early to go buy some pastries. It took me longer than I thought to find a bakery highly rated on Trip Advisor, so I stumbled into Lucy on the third floor of her building. She was running down the stairs. There's no doubt that New York is the city where everyone always rushes. I passed her a blueberry muffin as if I'd given her the baton in a relay race and blew her a kiss. When Lucy was on the second floor I looked down and told her that I was meeting Tony that evening at the Rainbow Café. "Strange," she said, but there was no time for small talk.

The day passed very quickly. It took a lifetime to see New York well, and I'd already lived half of mine. I spent the morning at the Metropolitan Museum. Since when did I like art so much? I did some more shopping in the afternoon and bought a yellow shirt with a small cactus embroidered on the chest. I wanted to look handsome for my date with Tony. I made it to the door of the Rainbow Café at 6:55 dressed in that shirt, beige chinos, and a camel-colored leather jacket. I was wearing the black briefs with the white stripe that Bernadette had given me "just because." They were very tacky, but she'd claimed they would bring me luck.

The Rainbow Café was gorgeous—a tropical garden, a greenhouse dotted with tables full of beautiful people. There were some mixed groups, and even a few elderly couples who had survived the Studio

54 times, but most of the tables were occupied by men. Everyone was dressed so *on trend* that I looked somewhat provincial in my cactus shirt. At 7:10 Tony hadn't arrived yet and I was starting to feel like an idiot waiting for him at the door. He was capable of standing me up.

Then I received a message:

"In the taxi. There in 5."

Not an apology. Nothing. I decided not to answer and wait until 7:20. If he had not yet made it by then, I would leave. I went inside to tell the restaurant we'd be a little late, but I didn't know Tony's last name.

"It must be this one," the waiter said and jotted something down next to one of the names on the second page of his list. I peeked to find out Tony's full name, but the waiter covered it with the first page, and I was kept from that privileged information.

"I'll keep your table for five more minutes," he added as if he had a stick up his ass. The moment I stepped outside again, a taxi stopped at the door. I stood up straight, sucked in my stomach, lifted my chin, and forced myself to smile. I was upset that he was late and nervous about where the date might go, but of course not in a million years would I go to bed with someone with HIV. I didn't even know why I had taken the condoms with me. I pictured the scene. Tony would get out of the taxi, smiling, and he'd look at me with a mixture of defiance and disdain, as if I had been late and not him. Then he would shake hands or, perhaps, kiss me, and I'd feel his chest against mine, and his smell would trigger my passions once more. I'd forget that I was angry, and I'd feel that lightheadedness again, maybe signaling the dawn of love. What did Tony have that made me feel that way?

The taxi door opened, his fingers clutched the edge of the door, and I still had time to think that I would not be putty in his hands when the one who got out of the car was John. He looked at me with his a-little-too-close-together eyes, gave me a warm smile, and put his hands together as if saying, "Sorry." I opened my mouth, but I think said nothing, and I ended up smiling at how silly I'd been. I waited, my hands in my pockets, for John to get his change back and come to me in two strides, with that enviable determination that I lacked so often.

"I'll make up for being late," he said to calm me down.

We were led to our table by the same waiter I'd talked to before. He had us sit at a corner table surrounded by small palm trees and orchids, and handed us the menu. The room was stuffy. Not the best weather for my cactus.

"I hope you don't mind meeting in a gay restaurant."

"Absolutely not. It's a beautiful place."

"I know the owner," he added. "He's a dear. If he happens to be around today, I'll introduce you."

I started to look at John with different eyes. Until then, I had focused on finding a resemblance to Michele, but now that I could reasonably infer that he was gay, our meeting took on a whole new dimension. I cared less whether his way of speaking reminded me of Michele's and more if I liked what he said and how he said it, if his vocabulary was cultured, or if he paused the conversation at the right time and gave me room to answer. In this way, I discovered that John was a good listener and that he showed genuine interest in what I told him. He had this unhurried way of saying things, always leaving his sentences open-ended so that I could add a comma, a parenthesis, or an observation—my opinion.

I considered each part of him in more detail than during our unfortunate meeting in Chatham: his almond-shaped eyes, his curly eyelashes, and those thick boomerang-shaped eyebrows which gave him an expression of permanent awe. Whenever I said something nice about him, he took his eyes off me, suggesting a hint of shyness which I loved; or perhaps it was just modesty. I noticed the way he tilted his head forward to show his interest in what I said, and how he placed his hands behind his ears as if making a bowl with them to pick up each one of my words. He spoke slowly, choosing the right words and avoiding those which sounded pretentious or over complicated. He expressed complex ideas with simple vocabulary. He smiled often, not in Tony's excessive way but as if he were afraid to show his teeth. His incisors were slightly longer than average, making him look like a charming naughty boy, but he was very polite. He talked using short, calm body movements. When he wanted to emphasize something, he turned his hands over, exposing his palms.

The first thing he did was apologize for the dogs' attack:

"But your behavior was very suspicious."

"You haven't asked me out just to feel better about yourself, right?" I asked. Then I got closer and whispered that I loved the place he'd chosen. John opened his eyes big and replied:

"Here they have anything you may want from an old fashioned to a mango margarita."

"I'll have a mango margarita then, with a little umbrella like that one," I said, pointing to a cocktail sitting two tables away.

He waited for the drinks to arrive before continuing the conversation.

"I'd like to meet Dawson after all." He took a sip. "But I couldn't find him." Apparently, he'd been unsuccessful searching for him on the internet. "Are you sure it's Dawson?" he insisted.

At first, I didn't know how to help him, but then I remembered Michele's brother, Patrick. He was the editor of *Wines of the World* and, bingo, the magazine was headquartered right there in Manhattan. So it'd be relatively easy to contact him and ask him to put us in touch with his nephew Dawson. I could even get his email address right then. I was sure I had it somewhere in my work folders.

"Would you do that for me?" he asked, showing his lovely incisors. He was very cute when he smiled, so much so that I felt like kissing him.

As I'd thought, it only took me a couple of minutes to find Patrick's info in my phone: p.keller@winesoftheworld.com

"Wonderful," John said.

We discussed the message I was going to send Patrick. John started to get excited at the prospect of meeting Dawson. It was quite a drastic attitude change since he'd kicked me out of his house. That day he hadn't wanted to hear anything about him.

When I questioned him, he reasoned that the death of his parents—or as he called them, John and Martha—in a car accident a little less than a year ago had left him with no other family besides a cousin in Minnesota.

"So you're alone in the world," I said paraphrasing Michele.

"I guess you could say so," he replied sadly. "I decided that I don't have anything to lose after all."

I would have liked to tell him more about Dawson, but Michele had always been very elusive, and I didn't want to make up anything. It'd been obvious from the beginning that Dawson was a painful topic, so I'd never been too insistent, except when I'd wanted to hit her where it hurts in the course of one of our squabbles. I had only seen, for a few seconds on the day we'd met, that photo dating back to when Dawson was a kid riding a bicycle, and that was only because it had accidentally dropped from her bag. The other times Michele had referred to him were just to mirror my recitations of Christine's pre-teen adventures. These were mostly generalities about the education of children, things that could apply to anyone. The truth is that Dawson was a complete stranger.

The more I talked to John, the more I felt an urge to help him. I had a sense that something tied us together beyond the omnipresent Michele. Her memory was fading quickly with my second mango margarita. John emerged from my misty past with his serene gaze, his calm demeanor, and those charming Transylvanian incisors. How different he was from Tony! No edges. No shadows. And so clean-cut what-you-see-is-what-you-get. I finished typing the message to Patrick on my cell phone and slurped the last drops of tequila out of the ice.

What if besides kissing I let him bite my neck?

John sat for a moment next to me, and I read the text aloud to get his approval:

"Dear Mr. Keller," I cleared my throat before continuing. My arm and John's were touching. I could feel his body heat through my shirt, and his short breathing practically in my ear. I kept reading:

"My name is André Broussard and I work at Junot Cellars (my boss is Mr. Picard). I had the pleasure of befriending your sister Michele after a visit she paid to us a few years ago. I am very sorry for your loss. It has been a great loss for everyone who knew her. Before she passed away, she asked me to do her a favor involving your nephew, Dawson, and that's why I need to get in touch with him as soon as possible. Would you mind providing me with his e-mail or a cell phone number where I can reach him? You can answer this email or call me at 011337348738. I will be in New York until Thursday. Sincerely yours, André Broussard."

John approved, so I sent the email.

"*Alea jacta est*," I said.

Since Americans don't take Latin, I had to translate that as the die was cast. Now we just had to wait for Patrick to answer the message because I couldn't think of another way to find Dawson. This seemed the shortest path. I had just asked John what he would do if Patrick Keller put us in touch with Dawson when the phone rang. Without thinking, he grabbed my hands.

"That was fast," I said. I would have just stayed like this for ever, feeling his skin on my skin, but with a look he motioned me to answer, so I took my hands from under his and answered the call. It was all a bit strange, as if we had realized at the same time that we didn't want to let go of each other.

"Let's see, let's see ..." I whispered as I pressed my phone's green button.

At the other end of the line, a deep male voice asked me very seriously if he was talking to André.

"Patrick?" I enquired.

"Patrick?!" exclaimed the now undisguised voice. "Who is Patrick, you slut?" A few laughs followed.

John looked at me questioningly. I pushed the phone away from my ear and gave him an "I don't understand anything" look.

"You wouldn't be cheating on me, would you?" the mysterious caller said. "Didn't we have a date?" And he laughed again.

Only then did I realize who I was talking to. I'd started to think of something ingenious to say when John stood up to greet someone behind me, and I got distracted.

"Long time no see," I heard John say before some hands covered my eyelids, hands whose soft and slippery touch I knew well. I dropped the phone on the chair and grabbed the hands by the knuckles. A sharp aftershave scent kicked in. It smelled of ice, menthol, and excess. I felt a small bite on my earlobe and then an all too familiar voice whispered softly in my ear, as if he were undressing me:

"It's a small world."

What the hell was Tony doing there?

By the time I started to react, he was standing in front of me. Tony and John kissed and checked each other out from top to bottom. I was sure that they would have said much more if I had not been there.

"But ... do you know each other?" I managed to say.

They looked at each other again. They laughed as if they shared a secret. That made me frantic.

"Kind of," Tony said.

"We do," John added as Tony grabbed a chair and sat with us.

"When was the last time?" Tony asked nonchalantly and raised his fingers to get the attention of the waiter. Even that gesture was lascivious. He turned the wrist with the index and the ring fingers together, as if smearing butter on someone's butt.

"We have a friend in common," John said.

Tony stroked the back of John's neck. "I miss seeing you," he said. "And so does our friend."

John said nothing. He stared at his empty glass for a moment, just as absorbed as when he'd looked out to the garden the day before.

"But you guys are dry," Tony said, pulling his hair back. He looked at me for the first time that day and asked me:

"Would you like a gin & tonic?"

I watched them as they exchanged their impressions about the restaurant. Tony's hair was gelled, as at the Pink, and he was dressed all in black: tight V-neck t-shirt framing his very white face, shiny patent-leather shoes, and pleated pants giving him a slightly retro look. On the other hand, John looked like an office clerk on casual Friday, in his blue and yellow checked shirt and classic jeans. These two men were as different as night and day. Could I like them both? It seemed impossible, but then I thought—probably because they were sitting together right in front of me—that for a few hours at dawn when the air is grayish rather than blue, there is room in the sky for both the sun and the moon.

Then the phone rang, and John paid attention to me again.

"*Alea jacta est*," I repeated before answering. "Do you know what it means?" I asked Tony. It was Patrick Keller's secretary:

"Mr. Keller would like to know if you can meet him tomorrow at 10:00."

"Give me a second," I said. I left my cell phone on the table and hit the speaker button so that John could hear the conversation.

"At our offices on Lexington Avenue and 44th Street," she said. "Be punctual, please. Mr. Keller is a very busy man."

John and I spontaneously high fived, being careful not to be noisy. We were happy to be a little closer to finding Dawson. I completely forgot that Tony was there. My eyes focused on the joy and the undisguised satisfaction on John's face. He was more excited about finding his brother than he wanted to admit. His body language gave him away.

After the telephone conversation the waiter came to take our order.

"I'll stay with the mango margarita," I said. "I don't like to mix."

Tony didn't stay long. Once he realized he wasn't the center of attention and that we had a more serious matter to deal with, he made up an excuse and left.

"I have to go water the plants," he said, "but why don't we meet tomorrow, André? There's this great exhibit of a French painter, and we could snack something afterwards."

Watering his plants?

"It was just a joke," John said when we were alone. "Don't you know him?"

"Just a little. But you seemed to share good vibes."

John remained pensive for a little while. He was a thinking man. I was dying to know if there had been anything between them.

"Well, he knows you enough to invite you out," he said.

"You ...?" I insinuated, unable to keep it to myself.

"Are you kidding me? He's the Antichrist!" he laughed.

His response calmed me down. The possibility that John and Tony had had a flirtation, a crazy night, a bad screw or, worse, a good one, anything, just upset my stomach. "Why should I care?" I asked myself, already aware of the answer. I looked at John. The thought of him and Tony together made me sick.

"Actually, once," he retracted, "but that was a long time ago."

I tried to smile, but I just couldn't part my lips. That news had been a bucket of cold water—worse, a kick in the nuts.

How many gays could there be in New York? A hundred thousand? Two hundred thousand? Half a million? What were the chances of Tony and John having sex? Another thought struck me. What could the promiscuity rate be for that to happen? I had my head in the clouds. While I went back and forth like a fifteen-year-old between John and Tony, did half the city fuck the other half?

I didn't know what to do with my hands, so I sipped from my empty glass. John noticed.

"I'd buy you another drink, but I have to go now," he said.

"To water the plants?" I asked sarcastically. I was just crestfallen.

"I have a dinner appointment. A prior commitment, you know."

"Oh, I see," I babbled.

Just great, that was the last knife in my gut, even if it was a "prior commitment." I got up to say goodbye. I held out my hand, but he came and kissed me on the cheek.

"Thank you for this evening," he said from very close. "Call me tomorrow as soon as you are done with the meeting with Patrick. Okay?"

"Sure."

I stood for a while watching John leave for his appointment. If he turned around to look at me before going out the door of the restaurant, I still had a chance. Unfortunately, he crossed the street carelessly between the cars and got lost in the traffic. I felt a needle in my chest, as if the embroidered cactus on my shirt had pricked me.

TUESDAY

The next day I woke up early with a hole in my stomach. I'd been so naive the night before, the days before, my whole life really. "What made me think that John liked me?" I thought as I threw my "lucky" briefs in the hamper. For him I was just someone who was helping him find his brother, period. How silly of me, being head over heels sometimes for Tony and now for John, when probably neither one of them found anything special in me. Maybe I was in heat. How long since the last time I'd had sex? I weighed masturbating, but it just seemed impolite to do it at Lucy's house, so I brushed my teeth instead, with unusual force, as if I wanted to get rid of all the emotional tartar that I'd been accumulating since I'd landed in New York. I tried to focus on the day ahead, especially on the meeting with Michele's brother, but I couldn't help wondering what John had done after leaving me. Who did he rush to see? Where did they go? How did his evening end? It even crossed my mind that he'd run to meet Tony.

I unfolded the map of Manhattan. Lexington at 44th was quite far away, but if I left then I could walk and be there by 10:00. Before going out, I still had time to chat a little with Lucy, invite her to the musical on Thursday—my last night—and confirm what I already suspected: Tony showing up at the Rainbow Café had not been a coincidence. She reminded me that when I handed her the muffin on the stairs, I'd told her where I was going. She told Tony later.

"He cracks me up," she said.

"He surely does."

I didn't want to go into many details with her on how I felt. I'd been through too many ups and downs in just a few days since Michele's fateful news, and my response to so many stimuli hadn't always surfaced in the most orderly manner. Lucy noticed this unresolved tension.

"Just be careful, okay?" she said with round eyes. "You are both very important to me."

I decided I'd have an honest conversation with Tony that evening. No more games. I concluded that under his mask beat the sensitive heart that Lucy loved so much. Definitely. But that would be later. Now I had to go to the *Wines of the World* magazine headquarters in the heart of Manhattan, and I was running late. It was 9:50 when I arrived at the huge glass building where Patrick Keller had summoned me. According to the entrance hall business directory, his offices were on the tenth floor. When I left the elevator, the receptionist, a redhead in her thirties dressed in a charcoal gray two-piece suit, lilac blouse, and round tortoise shell glasses, gave me a de facto smile and invited me to sit down. She dialed a number and talked to someone. Then she made a face and hung up. She looked at me over her glasses as if I were a weirdo, picked up some papers from her desk, and disappeared through a back door. Soon after that, an African American security guard, big as a tank, asked me to accompany him. "Please, Lord, don't send another Hugo my way," I prayed.

"After you," he said quite coldly and followed me down a corridor that ran through the entire editorial department. It made me uncomfortable that he was on my heels the whole way. Along the corridor there were about twenty cubicles, almost all of them occupied. It was very noisy. Two telephones rang alternately without anyone picking them up, and some of the employees spoke to each other above the short dividing walls. How could anyone work in that madhouse?

When we arrived at the last office, the guard knocked on the smoked glass door. In golden capital letters was printed, "Dr. Patrick Keller." "Doctor of what," I thought as the guard opened the door halfway without waiting for an answer. We went into a huge office decorated in aluminum and glass. A funereal silence reigned. At the end of the office, a man between fifty-five and sixty with very abundant white hair for his age awaited me. His hair was perfectly trimmed and combed, as if he had just arrived from the barber. He wore an impeccable tailor-made blue suit and a maroon tie with a gold pin. He was sitting in profile behind a wooden desk, as if with one eye he was watching me and with the other he was controlling the city beyond the windows. He looked a little bit like Michele, although he was about ten, maybe fifteen years younger. He had the same incisive blue eyes, but his nose was wider and his lips thicker. The oval shape of his face was identical, widening at the height of the jaw. I was overwhelmed looking at a man who I somehow seemed to know. He was the only man in those offices with a view—and what a view it was. His office was silent. Only he had the power to break that silence.

"Thank you, Leroy," Patrick told the guard. "Sit down, please," he added and motioned me to a chair. Not a handshake, not a smile, nothing. My chair was significantly lower than his, but I made an effort to keep my back straight while I looked up at him.

"Well, how is our beloved Picard?" he asked coldly. I hadn't talked to Picard since Thursday when I'd asked him for a few days off to take this trip.

"You know him, always with new projects."

Patrick rehearsed a shy smile.

"He thinks highly of you, André," he said while looking at some sort of a file. "He says you are a good employee, honest ..."

So he had talked to Picard? When? It had to be today. If making me come in person was odd, checking my references was insulting.

"Then he will have told you himself how he's doing." I wasn't going to let him intimidate me.

Patrick smiled defiantly. "He also described you as a sensible man. Do you think of yourself as a sensible person?"

"I'm so sorry about Michele." I didn't know where he was going, but I wasn't there to get his psychological assessment.

"That's why it shocks me," he said, gradually raising his voice, ignoring my condolences. "Honest, sensible people don't come up with such tall tales." The last word sounded like a punch on the table. I turned to look at the door. Leroy blocked the exit, which didn't look very promising, but then Patrick told him to make the rounds. When he left, Patrick leaned back in his chair and said:

"Michele had no children, Mr. Broussard. She was married for more than thirty years, but the Lord was not willing to grant her that gift."

The floor sunk from under my feet. It could not be. It simply could not be. Had she been lying to me all that time? But why?

"But she told me she did. And I saw a picture," I protested.

"God knows that my sister had an overflowing imagination, but she was not a liar, Mr. Broussard."

"I agree!" I said a little too loudly perhaps, my body tilted forward.

Leroy re-entered. He'd made the shortest rounds ever. I swear he could see through the walls. Patrick was looking at me with his piercing blue eyes.

"That's why I don't understand it," I added conciliatorily.

Patrick glanced at Leroy, and the guard took a step toward my seat. "I wish I had her letter," I thought, but I'd left it in Strasbourg.

"I am sure you came in good faith. I am convinced that a misunderstanding lies at the core of this whole issue. I wouldn't have bothered to ask you to come if you hadn't mentioned Dawson in your message."

I was missing something. It didn't help that Patrick spoke with the same stilted lexicon as Michele. They had certainly grown up in the same milieu.

"I already told you that Michele showed me—well, she didn't exactly show it to me but I saw—a picture of a child. It dropped from her bag—the picture, I mean. She told me he was her son and that his name was Dawson. You may believe me or not, but I haven't made this up."

Patrick interrupted me:

"When I was little, my family had a house in North Dakota."

"What the hell do I care?" I thought. That sounded like the beginning of "Out of Africa."

"A farm, right?" I said, recalling one of my first conversations with Michele: the horses, Portento ...

"We had already moved to New York. We hardly went there anymore. It wasn't an idyllic place. My parents threatened to send us there when we misbehaved. That's how bad we thought it was."

Patrick turned around in his chair and stared back at the city. I could see his face reflected in the windows and, beyond the glass, the warrens of office buildings on 44th street. He closed his eyes.

"Michele spent a long season in that house once. I was a child and did not understand her absence. I missed her." He opened his eyes again. His voice was deep and serene like that of a radio broadcaster. "The farm was in the middle of nowhere, almost an hour from the nearest town on a dusty road."

I didn't stand a chance of talking. Patrick controlled the room. I decided to shut up and let him dust off what looked like a family secret. Then he turned around and looked me straight in the eye:

"Do you know what that town was called?"

I shook my head. How could I know? "I neither know nor care," I would have told him if Leroy had not been there and if my work at the cellar didn't demand I behave exquisitely with Mr. Keller. This wasn't going well. I wanted to send that stuck-up jerk packing. To hell with Michele, with John, with Tony. Fuck New York, definitely fuck North Dakota. Who had heard of North Dakota anyway! I was tired of enduring humiliations, attacks by dogs named after children's tales, and threats by violent neighbors. I was sick of feeling horny and never getting any. What would come next? I was tired of everything and everyone.

"Dawson, Mr. Broussard. That shit-hole town was called Dawson."

"Fuck *me*," I thought.

After dropping that bombshell, he thanked me with those Anglo-Saxon thanks that don't mean anything added by default at the end of each sentence and went back to his papers.

"Please send Mr. Picard my regards," he said to signify the end of our conversation. He raised his right hand, and Leroy walked me to the door of the office. I was about to leave with my tail between my legs, but at the last second I decided I wouldn't leave without saying what I thought, even if it cost me my job, so I turned around and added a final plea:

"So you don't care about what happened, Mr. Keller? Who was the boy in the photo? What was your sister really like? You really don't want to know?"

Patrick unhurriedly raised his head and with the dignity of a priest officiating a funeral, said:

"Michele is dead and buried. God rest her soul, and we keep her in our memories."

That's how "religiously" he dispatched me. His decision to dismiss me had some advantages. For one, it spared me having to tell Patrick that John existed and was his nephew, although I suspected he already knew. The only reason he had agreed to see me was as a courtesy to my boss. It had been just business for him. He didn't really care about what I had to say. My meeting with Patrick Keller had opened my eyes to something essential. It changed my view of Michele. I owed nothing to someone who had tricked me about something so vital, so I felt liberated. I walked down frantic 44th Street—my age, what a coincidence—feeling strangely somewhat optimistic, as I had after the incident at John's house. I was getting used to being kicked out of places. I just hoped Lucy would continue to let me sleep on her sofa. Maybe the trip to New York was about that, and there was a lesson to be learned from every kick in the pants, a moral in the middle of so much nonsense. After all, I had survived every rejection and had come out strong. But what about John? Would he be so optimistic? I worried he wouldn't take the news well. He'd allowed himself to become excited at the idea of having a brother. One thing I knew. I wasn't going to tell him on the phone that Dawson was a small town lost on the North Dakota plains, but I had also promised to call him after the meeting with Patrick. I didn't know what to do.

I joined the crowd going into the subway. I'd been completely stupid to let myself be dragged into Michele's whims. Had I made this trip to tell John about a brother who didn't exist? Impossible. Michele wouldn't waste my time just for the heck of it. What did John gain from all this? What did I gain? And above all, what did *she* gain? There was one thing I was sure of. Michele had genuinely loved me and wouldn't have risked ruining my memory of that love. Memories are the only things the dead leave behind. I was missing something, but I didn't know what. Maybe I should ask Samantha to go to my house, take some pictures of Michele's letter and send them to me by WhatsApp. She had Christine's keys, didn't she? Maybe the solution was where the problem started.

I needed some air and to feel like just another tourist for a while, so I decided to get off at Battery Park and take the ferry to Staten Island. The ferry supposedly offered the best—and cheapest—views of the skyline and the Statue of Liberty. Few people knew of the sculptor's Alsatian origin, but he even had his own museum in Colmar.

The boat was quite full of New Yorkers coming and going across the bay, as well as a sizable number of tourists. In the beginning, I kept myself busy with a fairly large group of kids about Christine's age who burst onto the deck, laughing and pushing. In front of me, three girls were seated on the knees of male classmates, licking heart-shaped strawberry lollipops and singing a song by Beyoncé. The boys talked amongst themselves and, from time to time, punched each other, playfully reaffirming their masculinity. One with fuzz on his upper lip pulled one of the girls' ponytails. She turned around and slapped him. Another of the boys took advantage of the uproar to make out with a blonde in fuchsia leggings. Everything seemed simpler in the days of sticky lollipops.

A couple of men in their mid-twenties threaded their way past the teenagers and asked me to take their picture. I framed the snapshot while they grabbed each other by the waist and put their cheeks together. "One, two ..." I counted, and before reaching *three*, they showed their hands to the lens. They were wearing matching titanium rings. "Cheese!" I said superfluously since they hadn't stopped smiling from the beginning. I took their photo, feeling envious of their happiness. I gave them back their camera and leaned on the railing. The water looked as thick as chocolate with the dim glow of lead and the iridescent and multicolored reflection of a thin layer of oil that floated on the surface. The air smelled a little like canned tuna. I wished we would move soon so that the current could mix the sludge with cleaner water.

As soon as we started moving, the tourists abandoned their lethargy and filled the deck to take snapshots of the skyscrapers. The breeze was waiting at the mouth of the dock. It ruffled my hair and filled my lungs with the thrill of adventure. I had read somewhere that a trip only begins when you leave the security of the port. I was unsure if that applied to me since I was just going to Staten Island and didn't even plan to get off the ferry. As we moved away, the city started to resemble a huge steel and concrete porcupine. The One World Trade Center tower stood out above the others in the same place the Twin Towers once stood, reflecting from its glass base the surrounding buildings and from its tip, the sky.

An elderly man in a gray suit and a bowler hat came and stood next to me. His face was large and square, possibly Russian. He looked as if he had lived all his life in a place other than the one he was from. He didn't speak to me, but he showed me a photo, taken on the very same boat, in which he was smiling next to a beautiful, plump woman. The image had been taken a few years before. He looked younger and happier, and the Twin Towers loomed like giant antennae over their heads. He moved his index finger from the photo to the horizon where the One World Trade Center now stood and then from the horizon to the photo. He did this three or four times. Then he stared at me with his small, glassy eyes that contained all the pain and the joy of the universe. He held two fingers in the air and then just one. I put my hand over my heart meaning "I get it." He put the picture away in his jacket pocket, his hand on his hat in farewell, and left. I kept thinking about the woman and the absent Towers that everyone missed. Where there were two standing proudly in the wind, now there was only one. My shadow stretched into the water, and my reflection looked like a cypress tree. The ferry splashed a fine salty drizzle which smelled like the foam of the waves on the beach after a storm. I recalled the broken smile of the old man who'd just left. I had only one thought. I didn't want to die without having loved.

The phone rang. It was John. "And?" he said without any preface. I couldn't hear him very well.

"Well," I replied, regretting taking the call. I had nothing positive to tell him, and I hated the idea of disappointing him.

"Any news? I've been restless all morning."

"I'm on a boat. Long story. I have no coverage. I'll call you later."

"Just tell me if you were able to talk to Patrick."

"I did. I talked to him. I wish you had come along. After all he's your uncle."

"What are you talking about?"

He was right. I was making things worse.

"Sorry, it's just not something I can tell you on the phone."

On the other side of the line there was an awkward silence.

"Would you like to meet? Where are you?" John asked.

I didn't know how to continue that conversation. I couldn't tell him without looking him in the eye that Dawson didn't exist, that he never had except in Michele's imagination. And while I really wanted to see him, I definitely didn't want to hear him talk about his other dates, much less imagine him hooking up with Tony.

"John? John?" I repeated as if I were losing him, and then I hung up.

Before I was invaded by guilt, I felt a momentary relief. On the foggy horizon, the silhouette of the statue appeared, holding the torch, starry crown on, defiant and proud on its pedestal. Would it be a man or a woman? From closer up it wasn't obvious. Man or woman, woman or man. Did it really matter? It was Liberty Enlightening the World. A bravo to the sculptor, my fellow Alsatian.

My cell phone screen lit up and immediately rang. It was John again. I couldn't continue my childish behavior. If he asked me, I would agree to a meeting. I cleared my throat and accepted his call after the second ring. Our talk was brief and focused almost exclusively on setting up our meeting. John suggested we meet that very same evening, but I had my date with Tony—just what I needed!—so John invited me to an early dinner in Chatham the next day.

"At your house?" I just wanted to make sure. I imagined climbing his steps without fear this time, careful not to step on the flowers. I saw myself ducking to avoid the ferns hanging on the porch and then passing the two rocking chairs on my left. The iron salamander watching the unwary fly seemed like a joke now. There were no dogs, no crazy neighbor in my reinvented paradise. I half opened the red door. I didn't have the time to peek inside—let alone enter—because the hellish squawking of a seagull brought me back to reality. I returned to the conversation, to the ferry, to that hard bench my knees were on, but it was too late. Desire had slipped in through the doorway during the short time I'd left John's door open.

"Don't get your hopes up," I said before hanging up, so that he could start to accept the bad news. Then I thought it had been a bit cruel to keep him on tenterhooks and then thought further and realized that my comment could also have a sexual interpretation in which case it would have sounded terrible. I was thinking too much. Our appointment had a clear purpose. But in a corner of my mind the idea festered that John could have suggested many more *innocent* places to meet: a bar, a park, the Brooklyn Bridge, or possibly a bridge without cars, fumes or noise, an anonymous bridge suspended in the haze like a swing and with the best views over the bay. Since he had suggested his house, I couldn't help but hear the vibrations coming from his bedroom on the second floor, a room I hadn't even seen. It didn't matter. I opened the red door again; I went upstairs; I dreamt of a large bed in the middle of the room, one with white sheets moving slowly like a cloud of milk on top of coffee and mosquito nets, like in the tropics, tied with large bows to each corner post. The fresh air from the garden below enters through the back window. The curtains sway slightly, wafting in the breeze. On the ceiling, a wooden fan stirs the smell of dew and freshly cut grass. Or even better, let's leave all of that out, let it be just the breeze cooling our skin.

That's how I spent the entire journey back from Staten Island, with a stupid look on my face asking for someone to slap me out of it.

Back at home, Lucy opened my eyes with her traditional wisdom.

"You've fallen in love!" she said as soon as I asked her what to wear the next day.

"No way!" I replied.

But her logic was overwhelming:

"How come you are asking me what to wear tomorrow if you have a date with Tony today?"

A big cock. It turned out he had a big cock. But let's take first things first.

I left Lucy's apartment at 6:30. The plan was to pick up Tony at his house at 7:00, go to the French artist exhibit and then have dinner near his place in Soho. I went down the stairs, taking two at a time. I wasn't quite sure why I had accepted Tony's invitation, nor why he had invited me, but he'd said it in front of John, and I hadn't known how to decline. I needed to get over this thing of always having to make a good impression. I still had a hard time saying no under certain circumstances. At first, I thought Lucy would be coming too. I didn't find out until later that she wasn't part of the deal and that she couldn't tag along either because of work, but by then my stupid sense of commitment forced me to keep my word.

"I'll have a good time," I thought when I first went outside.

I needed some fun after the letdown at *Wines of the World*, and you had to admit that Tony was a guy with a spark. A son of a bitch, but hilarious, you had to give him that. And above all, he was a good friend of Lucy. He had talked about her so very lovingly in the Pink! Although I hadn't liked the way he'd talked to me, it was commendable that he'd wanted to distract her and smooth things out for her in the hard times leading up to her diagnosis. Lucy was neither stupid nor masochistic. If she had him as a friend, there surely was a good reason.

I turned the corner by Geppetto's, the pizzeria where I'd had dinner two days before. I recognized the smell of melted cheese and baked pepperoni. Its red neon sign with a hand that turned on and off marked the limit of my domain. Beyond Geppetto's it was no longer my neighborhood. In my neighborhood, I had bought bananas and blueberries at the fruit and vegetable place located between the flower kiosk and the 7-Eleven where I got my M&Ms on my way to the subway. At Frank's, I'd bought prosciutto, mortadella, and a little brie. Manuel at the Piccolo Café fixed me a toasted poppy seed bagel with cream cheese on Sunday, and a couple of times he poured me a coffee with cream, no sugar. I only knew their names from the little tags on their chests, but for me that was enough. With so little time in the city, I'd done most things only once. The second time around, they were routine in my borrowed neighborhood.

I was only one block from the subway when I decided to take a taxi. Michele had given me a lot of money for this trip. I didn't have to continue traveling like in my student days. In fact, I could have stayed in a good hotel, but I did not like the yellowish light of the rooms, even in the best ones. I hated the loneliness of hotels because it reminded me of my own. Lucy's flat was priceless because it came with her inside.

I got out of the taxi on Canal Street, in the heart of Chinatown. The taxi driver pointed out an adjacent one-way street.

"Are you sure it's here?" I insisted. He didn't answer. He put his finger on the meter: twenty-three dollars. Soho was close by, but Tony lived in Chinatown. Even the McDonalds sign was in Chinese. I recalled Tony's exact words when I'd asked him where he lived. "Do you know Soho?" he'd answered. I guess it was me mistakenly associating ideas.

Tony lived in a recently restored brownstone. The facade looked very nice. Let's see the what the inside looked like. I rang the bell: 10-A.

"You are early. Come in," he said without asking anything else, and the door sounded like one of those fly electrocuting machines. I looked at the time. I was seven minutes late. I buzzed again. I wanted to tell him that I'd wait for him downstairs, but I heard the same noise, and the door released again. Then the click of him hanging up. I pushed open the door wishing it had been the red one. The hall had a chic air, maybe too much gold and too many mirrors, but that fit Tony like a glove. I personally thought that less is often more. At the end of the hall, the elevator was waiting for me, doors wide open.

I didn't go into Tony's apartment so innocently. I wasn't the little mouse getting into the cat's jaws inadvertently. I could have chosen not to go up. I could have rung the bell a third time and made myself heard. But this was one of those nights when you feel really good: handsome and relaxed. I was ready to do something that made me feel just a little badass. Alive.

The door was ajar. It was garnet. I opened it just enough to slip inside. The apartment was in the shadows, but you could see, deep into it, a part of the living room, dimly lit by a light that rose and fell in intensity: the light of candles. It reminded me of the flashing hand on Geppetto's sign shining on the passerby's faces—what nonsense.

"Tony?"

I took two steps down the hall. The steam of a recent shower still floated in the air. It smelled of incense and the scent of a soap. Jean

Paul Gaultier? Maybe not. It was probably just me looking for something from home.

"Hello?" I insisted.

I heard a melody, midway between fado and samba, enticing me to continue down the narrow hallway. I wanted to reach the room where the flickering candlelight came from. I wanted to get to the source of that seductive music, which spoke to me of dark skin, sweat, and sex. There where the scented smoke fled from the wax in a tray that in my mind was made of tin. I wanted to get where he who'd lit the candles was, he who had ignited the incense, the one who'd chosen that devilish song, that beautiful son of a bitch with the dark blue, almost black eyes.

I wanted the moon tonight, that night, but tomorrow, I wanted the sun.

As the air turned orange, the feeling that I was headed straight for hell swept over me. I just loved this purgatory! With every step I took towards the heart of Tony's apartment, I felt warmer and warmer, as if the fire was coming from a pyre and not from the candles—from the crackling wood, not from the silent wax. I threw the splinters of my fear of catching AIDS into the fire, together with my resistance to becoming a piece of inflamed meat. I burnt the dreamed of red door, and from the fire rose a ring of black smoke that barely smelled of John. I threw the André I wanted to be into the flames. The one I was remained: the simple fag with a racing heart and a mind obliterated by the joyful trembling between my legs. The checked tablecloth bistro lover André vanished. The banquet was now served hot and steaming in the room I was about to enter. Food and nectars were waiting for me, served on pink velvet.

Before I reached the end of the hall I stopped for a moment. I was pleased to feel my heart beating where it didn't belong, pumping blood a couple of feet down. I wanted to abandon myself to the slight dizziness and throw caution to the winds. I enjoyed recalling the sweet taste of past romances and dreaming of new ones. There was pleasure in delaying the inevitable a little bit.

Ahead the air moved, as if the candles had changed places. I entered the room. I looked to the right. Tony's face looked red from the light of the two-arm candlestick he held in his hand. His back was reflected in the mirror behind him. He was wearing a white tuxedo shirt, unbuttoned, and shiny gray dress pants. His hair was still wet. He approached me slowly, wearing a confident smile. The flames of his two candles danced up and down and had almost faded by the time we met next to the low table where the incense was burning.

"This time there is no turning back," he said and put one of the candles out with his fingers.

I lined up my hips with his. I grabbed his ass. The fire of the remaining candle heated my eyelashes and dried my eyes. I rubbed my penis against his penis through the pants. What a stupid protocol. I pulled his zipper down and his cock just bloomed in my hand, the flesh erect. I blew the second candle out, and I was left with the memory of Tony's half-open mouth. I ripped the candle holder from his fingers and reached down to put it on the table. I found myself facing his penis. It was beautiful and looking to get in my mouth.

"Suck it," he said, grabbing my hair and pulling my head close to his cock. It hit me first in the eye, then it crawled down my cheek and walked on my lips.

"Shut up," I said, barely resisting. I took it again. I felt the heat of his flesh in the palm of my hand with his mighty head.

"Come on, suck me off," he insisted, pushing. He entangled his fingers in a lock of my hair and twisted it. It hurt me.

"Shh," I whispered, my mouth watering.

"André, *s'il vous plait*," he pleaded.

When I heard that he'd named his desire André, I wet my lips, swallowed, and I ate it all.

It goes without saying that we never went to the exhibition of the French artist. I didn't even get to know his name. I suspected that Tony had invented everything. Who cared. I decided not to dig into his reasons. What for? I'd just had the best one-night stand of my whole life—wild, wonderful, a Bordeaux, not a Beaujolais. I put my all into it. I had given him everything. To him, to Tony, the person who probably least deserved it.

I spent several hours in his room that night and not all of them having sex. In addition to the feline lover, between his sheets that evening I discovered the smart and scathing conversationalist, and even the man able to get thrilled at the whisper of a beautiful word. Tony was all those things and many more.

At about 2:00 am we had nothing more to give each other and little to say. At that point, I knew enough about Tony to remake a memory of that night reasonably adapted to my principles. To know more would have been to know too much, and I didn't feel like spending the next few days hashing things over. I had enough with a brushstroke here and another there of that other Tony, a few golden reflections to soften an indisputable truth. We'd had sex for the mere pleasure of sex and nothing more. We'd been two candles burning before the wax ran out.

"I'm leaving," I said. I gave him a hurried kiss. I sat on the edge of the bed and put on my briefs. My penis ached rubbing up against the cotton.

"Are you, *mon amour*?" he replied carelessly.

I stood up and caught him finishing a yawn. The sheets covered his ankles, nothing else. I wished he'd say, "Don't go" or at least, "Stay if you'd like" but that was the way things were.

"Are you going to tell Lucy?" I asked him.

Tony burst out laughing and I had no choice but to smile at the naivety of my question. I kept dressing in silence.

"I had a great time," I said.

"Good."

Then he walked me to the door. He put his arms around my neck, very slowly, and gently rested his wrists on my neck. He then let them slip down like satin sheets. He looked at me sweetly with that blue of his eyes. He kissed me and stroked my cheek.

"Be careful out there," he said.

It sounded like, "Be careful today and always, be careful in life" or even like, "Don't go around fucking anybody like me." Indeed, I would never see Tony again.

It is not true that New York is the city that never sleeps. By the time I left Tony's apartment, most people were asleep—some in cardboard boxes—and so were their frustrations, their jealousies, and almost all their sins. Dogs, even feral cats slept. Birds slept, that's for sure, because there was not one single noise when I left Tony's building except the hum of the subway under my feet. It was that odd hour when it's too late for almost everything and too soon for the rest. Only cockroaches seemed to be animated. Right in front of Tony's door someone had stepped on one. It was as crushed against the sidewalk as a dried flower between the pages of a book. How did I not see it when I'd arrived? I kept walking down the street. There wasn't a single living soul, and that included my own. I had left mine stuck to Tony's back. Four or five garbage bags were piled up at corner of an alley. They stank of rotten fish, curry, tamarind, and a festering mixture of beer and coke fermented with soy sauce. If China smells like that, they can keep waiting for me to visit. A noise attracted my attention to one of the open trash bags. A rat stuck its snout into the head of a shrimp, picked it up with its legs, turned it around, and ate what it could, totally devoted to that second-hand feast.

I kept walking until I reached a wider avenue. Could it be Broadway? Nope, it was Lafayette. Why did I always feel so weird after a night of sex, as if I had done something wrong? Not necessarily bad but unworthy. I had been dragging that feeling since my teenage years, since the prehistoric times when Lucy got a perm, and she was something in between my girlfriend and a friend with benefits. Even then I felt that way every time I went back home after having sex at her house. And it kept happening. If it was after sunrise, I felt even worse, or the less I knew my partner, or the more intense my orgasm had been. It's difficult to explain what I felt: a vacuum from the waist up, an unease, the terrible hopelessness of walking half lost through life while the rest of the world was sleeping.

I was hungry. I had not eaten anything except for a bowl of cheerios during one of the breaks from having sex with Tony. I went into a Dunkin' Donuts and ordered a decaf and a blueberry muffin from the Brazilian employee. I was becoming addicted to mega muffins. I sat at a table by the window. Opposite me there was a dark brownstone, with some broken windows and zigzagging emergency stairs all over the façade that didn't reach the ground. What was their purpose then? I sipped my coffee. I burned my lips. "Should I sue them for a million dollars?" I took the wrapping off and swallowed the muffin in four bites, with the same unhealthy eagerness I had devoured Tony.

WEDNESDAY

I hardly slept that night. In the morning, I heard Lucy fiddling with the kitchenware. Eventually, she couldn't resist her curiosity and woke me up.

"Do you want to keep sleeping?" she said, sitting on the edge of the sofa. I covered my face with the pillow. I knew I wouldn't fall asleep again, but I didn't feel like telling her the nitty-gritty of my crazy night with Tony. It was embarrassing.

"Come on, *Misterpartyallnight.* It's already Wednesday," she insisted, and took the pillow off me. I opened my eyes and saw her comforting smile. "I've made coffee."

At breakfast, I tried to casually explain what had happened, but it was difficult for me to start talking. I had reluctantly told her I was gay just a couple of days ago, and there I was now, telling her that I had slept with her best friend.

"It's like taking the skin off a fish," she said rather frustrated at my slow narrative. "Just tell me you used a condom. Tony will tell me everything else."

She turned white when it took me a second to give her an answer.

"I'm not a fool," I said.

She looked at me for a long time, as if she wanted to add something else, or as if she were looking for the old André but couldn't find him. In the end, it was me who spoke:

"Great coffee. Thank you."

For a while, we both looked silently at our own cups.

"And now what will you do? Are you going to continue with Tony?" she finally asked.

"Do you mean if we are going to get married and have children?"

"I can't see Tony parenting," she laughed, "well, I'm not so sure."

"I'm going back to France the day after tomorrow, Lucy," I said.

Lucy smiled, her eyes on the coffee. It was a sad smile.

"Have you done everything you wanted to do here?" she asked, raising her eyes.

"I did what Michele wanted me to do, and I've seen you. I am satisfied." As I said this, I had a vision of Tony sleeping beside me with messy hair, and then another of John crossing the street, getting lost among the cars outside of the Rainbow Café. I wished it had been the other way around.

"It's sunny today," Lucy said as she stood up from her chair. "Do you have any plans?"

I did, and they weren't very pleasant. I reminded Lucy of my meeting with John to tell him about Dawson.

"It seems to me that you are brooding about this way too much. After all, John had grown up as an only child."

She opened the fridge and put away the butter and milk.

"What do you mean?"

"Well, it's not like he had a brother and he died or something like that. I think he's going to take the news much better than you are anticipating. He may even be relieved, if you want my opinion. Do you want a banana?"

Lucy was probably right, and I was overthinking it. But I still felt some restlessness, some pins and needles in my stomach.

"I think you're more nervous about seeing John than about what you have to say."

Lucy always hit the nail on the head, I thought as I bit into the fruit. It was perfect, neither green nor too ripe. When I looked at the banana to take the next bite, I saw that it was a little stained with blood. My gingivitis again. I looked at Lucy. She was still talking, but I wasn't listening. I had zeroed in on only one thought: AIDS.

That afternoon I took the 5:00 pm train to Chatham. I had wasted the morning obsessing over the same thing. Like a hamster, once I got onto a wheel, it was hard for me to get off.

"It's not that easy; it's not that easy; it's not that easy," I kept repeating like a mantra on the train, while looking time and time again at the bottle of wine I had bought for the occasion. I was holding it between my legs, wrapped in paper. The bottom of the plastic bag had broken at the station. I'd spent seventy-five dollars on a Domaine Ostertag Vignoble d'E that in France didn't sell for more than twenty-five euros, but I wasn't worrying about the money then. One of my worst and most recurring enemies was back, and its name was fear.

"How could I have been so stupid," I whined while trying to remember the statistical probability of getting AIDS through oral sex. I had looked it up once. I'd already been through that before. "And suspecting Tony had it ..." I had used protection for the hard stuff. I was an idiot but not a suicidal idiot. I knew there was little risk, but I didn't expect my gums to bleed. It hadn't happened to me in a long time. "Never again." Hadn't I said that before? If Tony was being treated, he could hardly spread it. Had I read such a thing? Or was it a comforting thought I'd just made up to calm my anxiety? I had to stop or else I'd start hyperventilating. I took several deep breaths, trying to empty my mind. Most likely, I wouldn't have gotten AIDS from giving Tony a blowjob. If so, half of New York would have it. As far as I recalled, my gums weren't bleeding the day before. I also didn't think he'd come in my mouth. Had I noticed anything?

"Stop thinking. Stop it!"

As if the driver had read my mind, the train stopped, and the doors opened. We were in Chatham.

As soon as I started to make my way to John's house, I calmed down significantly. It was hard to see shadows between idyllic single-family houses, flower beds, and leafy trees. Fortunately, my obsessions went as quickly as they came. Over the years I had learned to live with them. I had a method. First I'd let them run until I went crazy, sometimes to the point of wanting to throw myself out of a window for something that hadn't even happened yet. Then I would retrace my steps. I would ask myself what the worst-case scenario would be and all the other questions that I had learned to answer by reading piles of self-help books. I concluded that I'd better forget about it. The chances of contagion were minimal, but just to make sure I'd get a blood test in a few months.

The idea of seeing John was very enticing. I was tired from the late evening but very excited to see him. I found him sitting in one of the two rocking chairs, pensive as always, dressed in beige Bermuda shorts and a Yankees shirt. What a happy sight. He smiled at me, waved his hand, and slowly walked down the steps to greet me. He gave me a warm, totally unexpected hug. I closed my eyes and enjoyed the moment. He smelled so good ... Before he let go of me, he pressed me tightly against his chest. I was tempted to leave the bottle on the ground and return his affection, but he took my hands with the wine and brought them up to the level of his eyes to read the label. He had a warm touch, like a healer's.

"Thanks, André. You didn't have to bring anything."

I liked that he called me by my name and the way he had to pronounce the *r*. Maybe I was going crazy, but I had the feeling he'd been practicing how to say it correctly.

"I hope you like pasta," he said, holding the door for me. I went in, a little fearful of the dogs, but they were nowhere to be seen. Maybe he'd kept them in the garden. We went straight to the kitchen.

John filled a pot with water, and I put the bottle in the fridge. It needed to cool.

"You wouldn't have a sleeve, would you?" I asked while searching inside the refrigerator. He looked at me, puzzled. "For the wine, I mean." I looked at what he kept in the fridge. Not much: some bacon, ham, cheese, a couple of beers, and a tray with fresh ravioli on the shelves; on the door, milk and orange juice; in the vegetable tray, hearts of romaine, six or seven tomatoes and a zucchini; in the fruit drawer, three apples and two pears.

"Can you pass me the pasta and the cheese, please?" He showed me a bowl with green sprouts and cherry tomatoes. "I've made a salad too. I just need to chop some peppers and grate some carrot. Would you like a beer while the wine cools?"

I opened two beer bottles and offered to help him cut the vegetables. While he studied how to attack the green pepper, I began to cut the carrot in julienne strips. John had square hands and large nails, cut in line with the fingertips. I paused to look at him. He was concentrated on measuring the pepper against the knife edge. I giggled.

"What?" he said, looking up and smiling at me.

"Nothing, you look like a skilled carpenter or something. We are just making a salad, not an armoire. Would you please finish up cutting the stupid pepper?" I teased him.

He ignored me, took a sip of his beer, and began to cut it into thick slices of the same diameter, then in twin sticks, and each stick in little squares. They were so perfect that they looked like confetti for a party.

We finished cutting the veggies. We finished our beers. We opened two more. The water started to boil, the pasta cooked, and John still hadn't asked me about the interview with Michele's brother.

I waited until we were finishing the salad, and then I brought the subject up.

"You don't want to know?" I asked.

John wiped his mouth with a napkin.

"Of course I do."

"Since you didn't say anything."

I decided it was time to open the wine. That would give the thinking man a couple of minutes to sort his mind and decide what to say. I stood up and went for the bottle.

"I wanted you to be the one bringing it up," he said.

"How come?" I removed the protection from the cap with the tip of the corkscrew.

"I didn't want you to think that I had invited you just for that."

I stuck the opener into the cork. I started to spin it slowly. My heart was beating harder. I debated whether to keep it subtle or be more direct. By nature, I was inclined towards the former, but I was feeling more daring after the night with Tony.

"And what have you invited me for then?" I asked as I uncorked the wine.

John half opened his mouth but closed it without saying anything.

"When are you leaving?" he asked.

"The day after tomorrow. But I'm considering changing my ticket and staying a few more days." I stared at him. I smelled the cork intensely. "I still have things to do here."

I couldn't really extend my trip and miss work, but I thought John would treat me more affectionately if he thought I might stay longer. I came closer to him, holding the bottle by the base like an expert sommelier. I poured wine in his glass and helped myself to some.

"Let's talk about Dawson," I said, ignoring the signals John was sending to me—more than that, frustrating them. What was wrong with me? Tony's episode had upset me. I was acting like a child in bumper cars. It was that feeling of speeding up to hit your best friend's car right in the front, and just before impact someone else comes out of nowhere and crashes into you on the side, shooting you off in the opposite direction. You are left facing the wrong way, stuck between the parked or broken cars along the edge, and unable to free yourself no matter how desperately you spin the wheel, while your friend's car gets away. Then you just smash into the first car going by to get rid of the adrenaline rush.

"Okay, but first a toast, right?" he said, "here's to you changing your ticket."

I had already changed it. Not the plane ticket but the one with Tony, destination nowhere. Now I expected to get onboard John's train and didn't know how. The next few hours just flew by. I told him my meeting with Patrick point by point. Lucy was wise. John reacted exactly how she had predicted: calmly, with restraint and a hint of resignation. I loved that about John. He seemed to know the true importance of each thing. He didn't give an issue more attention than it deserved, but he didn't give it less either. This was in contrast to me. With all my ups and downs and back-and-forths, I often overreacted. Things were simple with him because he was uncomplicated. He lacked Tony's glamor and sophistication, and he didn't have his wild side either. But so what? Comparisons are odious. One was sharp, the other insightful; one histrionic, the other subtle; excessive, moderate; outward, inward; the Yin and Yang. If Tony was sex, John was ...

I put that out of my mind.

We went on talking about other things. I told him about my marriage, my daughter, and my issues accepting my homosexuality. I shared my fears, my obsessions and my scarce sexual experience. I told him about my wishes and my concerns, and the way I could go from elation to plain boredom in minutes. And, little by little, while telling him of my eternal quest to be happy, we got closer and closer until we ended up side by side.

"Come to think of it," he said, pouring me the last drops of wine. "What do you need to be happy?"

"Right now?" I wanted to shout "you," but I said, "What do *you* need?"

"Someone who loves me," he replied without hesitation.

"Don't we all want the same? But the world is full of ..."

"Of Tonys?"

I didn't expect to hear his name at that moment, and I made a face. John opened his eyes. Right then, he knew.

"He's quite irresistible, isn't he?" he said.

I refused to talk about him. "Do you think so?" I finally said.

He hesitated, then said:

"There was a time when I thought he was, yes."

"There was such a time for me too."

It was obvious that my time had been yesterday.

"And today?" he said softly.

"Today I'm here."

"And is this where you want to be?" He stroked my cheek with the back of his hand. I got goosebumps; my eyes got wet. A deep, non-sexual emotion was breaking through, and yet, somehow, I found myself aroused. Our sentences had become as short as the distance between our lips, and I placed my "yes" inside him. That was a long and tender kiss: a waltz of tongues and hearts, at our leisure, craving nothing—a round, quiet journey that ended exactly where it had begun.

"Any plans for later?" he asked me after the kiss.

"None whatsoever," I said, my eyes on his eyes. I wanted to take it easy, but I was also aware that my days in New York were coming to an end, and I had to speed up the things I wanted to happen. I liked John a lot. I liked him in the calm way I longed to love. Did it make any sense to act on that attraction? In a couple of days I'd be back in Strasbourg walking alone alongside the canals. What would John be then? A souvenir from Manhattan?

He made a move to kiss me again, but I stopped him.

"John, I ... I want to go slowly."

Such procrastination was ridiculous, but I needed to take my time, cement each brick before laying the next one. Or not. Maybe all this talking to myself was bullshit. Was I fooling myself again?

"We have all the time in the world to get to know each other," he said.

Did we? I looked at him, stopping at each one of his features. All were imperfect, and each fascinated me. His facial muscles were relaxed. That gave me peace of mind. I felt as if I had known him forever. For the first time since I arrived in New York, I didn't want to go home.

"Would you like to see my little corner?" he asked me and started toward the studio.

I didn't take his proposal casually. I was convinced that he would not let just anyone into the intimate universe of his painting studio. His invitation was an open door to a part of his soul reserved for only a few. So I took it as a compliment. I began to walk on the parquet floor knowing that I was walking a very significant couple of feet, and when I first stepped on the studio's ceramic floor, I knew that I'd just pierced the membrane separating the public John from the private one.

What would John the artist be like? For the time being, he was as patient and understanding as John the accountant who had accepted that he would have to wait for sex. I was the first victim of my own unjustified procrastination. I realized that. The day before, I'd had no problem boning Tony without standing on ceremony until I got a bellyful. I had just smashed my obsessions, one at a time, until I'd crushed them like the dead cockroach at the door of his building. I couldn't help comparing my staged arrival at Tony's apartment with the perfectly natural entering into John's studio. I was beginning to understand why I behaved so differently with John. With both Tony and John sex was around the corner, but the two lovers were polar opposites. Tony burned as fast as the candle wax that had welcomed me into his theatre. Like oxygen in contact with a single spark, he produced a colorful flame and gave off an ephemeral heat. On the other hand, John's canvases required time and patience, not just a chemical reaction. The nuance of permanence was important. John was an artist; Tony was an arsonist. Both had different ways of turning their energy into something else.

And I, as John told me next, was at first a blob of paint to him.

It took me a little bit to understand that it was a compliment. Rather, it seemed an insult. A blob of paint! I am not a painter, but I am not completely uncultured. I knew almost nothing about Impressionism, which turned out to be his favorite style. Monet, Degas, Renoir; he spoke a little about each one of them, and when I snapped at him, "What do you mean, a blob of paint?" he reached out to the art books that rested on the bench, grabbed a beautifully illustrated one, and eagerly turned the pages until he came up with a picture of a Renoir painting, one where a woman and a child walked through a flowery field. "They are his wife and son," he clarified. I knew that painting. I had seen it at the d'Orsay.

"Look at these flowers," he said, and held the book open before my eyes. "If you look at them from very close they are just red spots, just an impression." He was right. "But if you walk away ..." he added, taking a couple of steps back.

"They are poppies," I alleged.

"Exactly!" John smiled. "It took me a couple of days to see you; who you really are, I mean. But I did, André. And once you've seen them as poppies, they are forever that, poppies. It doesn't matter if the same red spot, on another canvas or to someone else's eyes, is a rising sun." He sighed. "And there goes another question: What turns those brushstrokes into flowers?"

I squinted, a little lost.

"Don't you think it's the green, grassy field around them?" He slammed the book and began to laugh out loud. "Sorry, I'm going over the top. How about we open another bottle?"

He had nothing to be sorry about. On the contrary, it was wonderful to realize how that seemingly normal man was no ordinary man.

We went back to the living room. We took our almost empty glasses with us and sat on the sofa. My resistance was about to be overcome by alcohol. One more glass would tip the scales in favor of *carpe diem.*

"First, I have to tell you something," I said.

"If it's about Tony, you can spare me."

Had he said that to show empathy or because he already knew everything? It hurt to think that they'd shared a bed, but it wasn't the right time to talk about it. The time would come, had to come, if this turned into something else. I smelled the wine that was left in the glass. I wanted to get rid of Tony's aftertaste.

"It's not about him, John."

"Perhaps you have a secret?" he teased me.

I responded with a half-smile. "It's about Michele."

John realized that it must be something important and concealed his impatience.

"If you feel like sharing it, I'll listen to you. If you prefer to forget it, you don't have to tell me anything. I have already made up my mind regarding you and I won't change it."

That was exactly what I needed to hear. Michele could have said those very same words just as convincingly. Was personality genetically transmitted? I remembered her way of loving me as I was, her unconditional support, our travels around the world, and her sometimes impossible, sometimes delightful temper. I remembered vividly the last time we met in Barcelona. I wanted to talk to John about that before kissing him for the second time. We both knew that the next kiss would send us to the point of no return.

"*Alea jacta est*," he said, "I've already put my bet on you."

"He's learned the Latin words, how cute," I thought. His determination and courage were admirable. We'd just met, and he was already betting on me? Those were big words hiding bigger feelings. Too early? Probably, after one single kiss, and yet they didn't sound at all premature. I also bet on him, on us. At the very least, I was resolved to try.

I hesitated. I could still make something up; change the story I was going to start telling him a second ago or sweeten it. After all, Michele was "dead and buried." Her brother Patrick's words reverberated in my mind. My fear was that John would change his mind once he learned what happened in Barcelona between his mother and me on that weekend long ago. John crossed his legs and looked at me with curiosity, but I couldn't discern whether he was just pretending to care or he didn't want to offend me by saying, "I am not the slightest bit interested." I was probably complicating things unnecessarily, anticipating an exaggerated reaction on his part. He'd only shown signs of calmness. I took a sip of wine and set my glass down. I stroked his knee and asked him:

"What do you know about Michele?"

I wanted to start from the beginning. Build things up slowly. I noticed an involuntary movement in his leg, but it was only a reflex in the face of a question that hurt him way more than he was willing to admit.

"Nothing," he said, not looking at me. "I already told you she was more like a shadow."

He waited a few seconds, measuring the words he wanted to say next. Then he looked at me:

"Wasn't it you who had a story to tell me?"

He rested his hand on my leg. I stroked it. I would have caressed every patch of skin he'd put within my reach.

"Do you know what she told me once?" I asked. "That to love someone you have to know him."

"That's the honest-to-God truth," he replied immediately, his eyes on mine. I'd intended to convey the idea that he had judged her too quickly, and I had achieved the opposite effect.

"I did know her," I said.

He looked resentful, but it didn't last.

"And did you get to love her?" That sudden curiosity told me he wasn't completely indifferent to Michele. He could still see her with new eyes.

I took my time to respond. I didn't want to devalue the love that I could offer him. If I answered too quickly, perhaps he'd think I loved too easily, or just about anyone, or that my love was cheap.

"I struggled, but I did."

"You were going to talk to me about Barcelona."

"I'm going to tell you about Barcelona," I said, determined to open up my heart to him. I didn't want to keep secrets. John had to know them and forgive me, if there was anything to forgive at all. Things were going so fast, especially inside me. In order for me not to forget anything important, I had to remember the entire trip, from the very moment of Michele's invitation. Finding the words was relatively easy, but it took me a little longer to revive the mood I was in at the time.

"You may not like what I tell you," I warned John.

I sat closer, which forced him to uncross his legs. I didn't want to keep any distance. He also inched in. I ran a finger down the back of his neck. He closed his eyes and gave in to my caress.

"I felt totally different then from how I feel here and now. Do you understand?" It was only when I said that out loud, that I realized how far I'd come in the last months. It'd been a gradual change which had crystallized in New York in the light of all the situations I'd faced. I wish John understood how I felt each time, that my reactions were conditioned by their context. Now I was a different person, stronger, and slightly more self-confident. I breathed deeply. Could I make him understand that one always acts according to the circumstances?

John looked at me with enviable serenity. Maybe the only reason he was paying so much attention to me was so that I could vent, but I loved his respect, and the calm he gave me. Where did I get that stupid need to clarify everything?

I didn't know where to start, so I chose the trigger. I started off with the Spring of two years ago. Almost all the dates on the April kitchen calendar were filled with the usual notes, circles, and cross-outs. I am the old-school type—paper and ink, that kind of thing. I was washing the dishes when the phone rang. It was Michele, telling me that she had booked a last-minute Mediterranean cruise with some friends. Her ship left from Barcelona in fifteen days. Things happened more or less like this:

"Barcelona is not very far from Strasbourg, is it, André?" Michele said, disguising as a question what was, in reality, an assertion.

"For the rich everything is close," I thought. I suspected she had bought that trip to see me, but I didn't know how much was true in my guess and how much was my own conceit.

"Relatively," I said, holding my cell phone between ear and shoulder, and opening one drawer after another looking for a dish towel to dry my hands.

Sometimes I was a bit cruel to Michele. I knew how much she hated when I wasn't precise, and I played that card to test my power over her. With time I had learned how far I could go, and I experienced some satisfaction in driving her crazy every so often. I wanted her to lay her cards on the table. If she wanted to see me, she'd have to spell it out in full.

"Relatively far or relatively close?" she asked, and before I could answer, she added, "Don't you think that distance is a state of mind?"

I understood right away she was asking me to accept seeing her without sounding pathetic.

"I'm considering arriving a couple of days before the cruise starts," she finally admitted.

I didn't answer. At that time, I was starting to consider our excessive closeness a problem. I had become so accustomed to her presence on a day-to-day basis, we talked so much and so often that my emotions mixed with hers, and I practically lived for her. Due to the nine-hour difference with San Francisco, my nights were her mornings, and many times I was under the impression of living neither here nor there but somewhere on the Atlantic Ocean where the sun never set.

"Think about it. I would like to see you but if you can't, I will understand."

"Ok. I'll think about it," I replied.

"I am in a bit of a rush."

It bothered me that she applied additional pressure whenever she saw a loophole.

"I would have to book another hotel room for you. You will like it. Early 20th century, totally your style."

"I'll think about it," I repeated.

"I miss you. Remember that I love you," she said before hanging up.

As if she were going to let me forget. Wasn't that very same love also the yoke with which she controlled me? I would not go. I needed air. Time. A space free of Michele. I needed to concentrate on my work, which was what paid the bills. On Christine, who was then in high school and needed more supervision. Her grades had suffered since she'd started to hang out with Mathilde, her zombie looking "cool" friend. But above all, I urgently needed to focus on me, on my most intimate self, that guy who languished after 5:00 pm and always left a personal life for later. On that Saturday in May when Michele proposed that we meet, Bernadette had set me up on a blind date with some Maurice: lawyer, forty years old, divorced with two children. Bisexual. I had it marked with a red M on the calendar. She had tried him first, so he came highly recommended. I'd been able to stop Bernadette in time, before she went into greater detail. I wanted to go on that date. How many opportunities had I had? At that time, not many. The time had come for me to give sex a different face than that of François.

"Coward," I told myself while searching for flights to Barcelona on my laptop. For some reason, I'd rather surrender to Michele's "safe" love than to address my issues.

I tried to explain to John that the problem back then wasn't so much accepting my homosexuality as knowing what to do with it. It was as if someone had put in my arms a huge, colorful box labeled "gay," told me, "I'll be back in a sec" and had never returned. Inside the box I'd found some golden packages filled with black stones representing the things that bothered me about myself. I had little appreciation for my body and a visceral fear of getting sick. I didn't fit in that universe of seeing who has a bigger one or showing off your biceps. I could not understand that all the complexity of the cosmos was summed up in being active or passive.

"There are as many types of gays as there are human beings," John intervened. Nothing could be more true than those few words he said.

I kept recapitulating.

There were good tickets to Barcelona. It was tempting to accept her invitation, but was it good for me? Was it in my best interest to spend that luxury weekend in Spain? I was beginning to understand that it wasn't, that the time for those trips was running out. I had to find the happiness in my daily life, in the little things, in my routine. I had to travel inside me, seek the love of a man—perhaps Maurice—and loosen the emotional ties with Michele. Even breaking them didn't seem like a crazy idea anymore. But despite all that thinking, I pressed the "buy" button.

John understood that I had met Michele when I was most lost. She had picked me up when I least loved myself. He realized that she'd given me the love I lacked but on an industrial scale. She'd offered it to me unconditionally and, to improve my self-esteem, she'd supported me in absolutely everything.

"Who doesn't need love?" John said timidly.

Michele placed me at the center of her life. It's nice to be in that place! Then she patiently wove a thick spider web whose threads only held as long as my emotional shortcomings continued to exist. In her defense, I will say that she was never tempted to undermine my self-esteem despite knowing very well that I'd need her less and less the stronger I felt. Keeping it low would also keep me more attached to her. Michele's intelligence never belittled that of others, and that included me. She knew I wasn't the type of person who submits to someone who holds out her hand after she's taken away the ladder. I wasn't weak that way. On the contrary, she always wanted me to feel better, stronger, happier, even at the risk of losing me. I never had the slightest doubt that her wishes were genuine, and that's how she won first my admiration, then my loyalty, and ultimately my love. She said, "you're handsome, you're smart, go conquer the world." She told me, "I love you just the way you are," not even quite knowing who I was deep inside. She said all the things I needed to hear. I knew she truly believed them, and yet, sometimes, I preferred to think of her as a snake in the grass.

"To know you is to love you," said John.

"Funny you'd say that. Do you know that Michele used to say the same thing?"

He got serious. He hadn't appreciated my comment. He didn't want to have anything in common with Michele.

I leaned over to get my drink and kept talking. My mouth was a little dry, and it would only get drier the deeper I went into my story.

"When I arrived at the Barcelona airport, I took a taxi. I had a small carry-on with just enough things to spend two days in town."

"Very good taste," the driver replied when I asked him to take me to the hotel Casa Fuster. The taste was Michele's and so was the credit card, but the driver didn't need to know. Michele was right when she'd told me that I would like the hotel. She knew me well. The entrance—in what used to be an old carriage access—was covered with bright mosaic, as black as a moonless night. The columns had flowers on the capitals and joined each other with wide arches that looked like upside down Venetian gondolas. On the right, a staircase of white marble climbed towards the upper floors. The metal filigree held the wavy railing. To the left was the bar, with mauve velvet seats harmoniously placed between a grove of modernist columns.

The smiley concierge announced that "my friend" had already arrived and handed over her note: "I am in room 409," followed by Michele's unmistakable signature, the *h* and the *l* tall like cypresses. Why did she sign absolutely everything? I was in room 410. The tradition of adjoining rooms was kept to the letter.

I went up to my room. I brushed my teeth. I washed my face. I don't know why I worried so much about smelling good. I emptied my carry-on. I hung one of the two shirts in the closet and left the other on the bed for ironing. Michele had accustomed me to these little luxuries. Then I called her.

"I made it. I need ten more minutes," I said despite being ready. I was a little angry at myself for setting out on that trip. We had seen each other quite recently, and I couldn't resort to the same logic I'd used to justify my other trips with her. This wasn't a chance for me to see some wonderful, beyond-my-reach place. I'd been to Barcelona several times. Much to my regret, I had to admit that I was there to see her. I let twelve minutes pass. Then I knocked on her door. She opened it barefoot, like the night of our dance in the rain in South Africa. She wore a green blouse and emerald earrings that heightened the blue of her eyes. She hugged me tightly but backed off quickly because I didn't hug her back in the same way.

"I missed you," she said. "Do you like the hotel?"

"Very pretty."

Her room was similar to mine. A book rested on her bed: *Love in the Time of Cholera*, English edition. I hadn't read it, but the title struck me. It must not be easy to love in such adverse circumstances. It should be way easier in a "time of plenty." Right?

"Did you have a good trip?" I asked.

"You need a drink," she said.

She'd clearly noticed my slight hostility. Did I disguise my feelings so poorly?

She invited me to sit on the sofa and went to the bathroom. "I thought we could have a drink at the bar before the concert," she yelled.

"Concert? What concert?"

"I have been told not to miss the Palau of the Catalan Music. Spanish Guitar. Do you feel like it?"

I looked at the time: 7:00 pm. I didn't give her an answer.

She came out of the bathroom, her lips painted carmine, mascara on her eyelashes.

She reached down to her two-inch wheels and put them on.

"So what do you think?" she said, spinning around. I raised my right thumb. She smiled, pleased. I smiled back at her. A part of me was really glad to see her—the part desperately needing love.

I looked at John before continuing. I didn't want to bore him. His eyes were a little wet. Was he moved by discovering my emotional fragility?

Michele and I had a glass of cava at the hotel bar, in one of the mauve chairs I had noticed at check-in. We were alone. We told each other everything we already knew. Neither of us cared. I like hearing the same stories from my loved ones. I always notice a different nuance. The plot changes every time we remember it. We were on our second glass of cava when a jazz quartet and a black singer in her mid-thirties arrived. She was a southern beauty with a smile as white as the big pearls in her necklace. Aretha—such is the name I gave her before she introduced herself as Fiona—proudly displayed her plump body, squeezed into a close-fitting black chiffon flared dress to her mid-calf. She had tiny feet for such a big body, or perhaps her patent leather shoes were a size too small. She sipped water from a plastic bottle, not in line with the elegant feeling of the place nor her own.

While the musicians were preparing to play, the room began to fill up with other hotel guests: six or seven elderly couples and a couple of men in their fifties, one of whom wore a bow tie. When the band seemed ready to start, the "ostrich family"—legs too long or body too short, or both—came in. It consisted of parents and their two teenage children, a boy and a girl, both redheads and way too old to be dressed as if they were going to take their first communion. They sat at a table on the other side of the small platform that served as a dance floor.

Michele suggested ordering a bottle of cava, and I encouraged her by saying, "Sure, why not!" She patted my hand and cheered up at the prospect of listening to the kind of music she liked best. There would be no time to finish the cava if we wanted to get to the concert, but since I didn't have a special interest in going anyway, I objected nothing and instead called the waiter. I was sure that Michele knew what she was doing. If we ended up not going to the concert, it wouldn't be by mistake. She wasn't one to overlook things like that, unless of course, she did on purpose. So we ordered that bottle of cava. Fiona didn't take her eyes off us and did not hide it. Whenever our eyes met, she gave me a huge smile. The waiter, a very ugly but very kind guy with a huge Adam's apple, took away the empty glasses and brought new ones. He ceremoniously placed the ice bucket beside me and uncorked the bottle. The cork shot out. He apologized, embarrassed. It was a careless mistake, but I liked the festive noise of the explosion. It reminded me of the bang which starts the show just before the fireworks. I looked at Michele. Her chin was up. She was showing perfectly lined up teeth. While she waited for her sparkling wine, her bright emeralds reflected in the glass she held in her hand, and I wondered whether she was the best person or the least appropriate one with whom to spend that evening of jazz and cava.

"Can I ask you a favor?" she said, raising her glass.

"Anything you'd like," I replied recklessly.

"Don't steal my bubbles tonight, ok?"

I laughed, as I always do when I don't know what to say, and also when I don't want to say anything. The static of the microphone came to my rescue. I looked up and once again was welcomed by the smile of that New Orleans beauty with the wide hips.

"*Buenas noches*," she said in a husky voice and a strong American accent. "Good evening," she added more confident now. She tilted her mouth and got closer to the microphone, as if she were going to kiss it. When I thought she was going to start singing, she looked up and winked at me, or I'd swear she did. With her index finger she drew the infinity sign in the air, and then sang her first song:

Me and Mrs. Jones
We got a thing goin'on
We both know that it's wrong
But it's much too strong
To let it go now

At the end of the chorus, she waved to the audience and then to the rest of the musicians, who nodded humbly. Fiona sang the way angels must sing along the Mississippi. She was all blues. She probably felt playful to have chosen that as her first song that evening, among the hundreds she probably had in her repertoire. The lyrics were priceless. Michele swayed, her eyes closed, and repeated every word in a whisper. Her voice didn't allow her any more frills. While Fiona spelled out every feeling, I questioned them all. Was there anything between Michele and I? If there was: how strong? how wrong?

After "Me and Mrs. Jones," Fiona wove each song into the next. Michele knew them all.

At the beginning of each one, she told me the title and the original singer, and sometimes she referred to some personal anecdote related to the song they were playing. I was hardly familiar with some of the artists' names and all but the most popular choruses, but I was happy watching her have a good time. From time to time, she came out of her reverie, stared at me, and recited the lyrics as if they were words of her own invention. She asked that we go together to the moon. "Fly me to the moon," she whispered. As if it were that easy. With each song and with each glass of cava, I found myself happier and happier to be spending that evening in her company. That world of heavy curtains, waxed floors, marble baseboards, and velvet seats suited me. I loved all the decadent elegance. Maybe that's why I liked Michele?

"Love me or leave me," Fiona said announcing the next song.

"That's wh[…]" John interrupted me sweetly. I didn't have time to answe[…] it, he put his fingers on my lips. He […]ase the words that still floated in the[…] us. I closed my eyes and felt his ton[…] frolicking in my mouth. Immediatel[…], on my neck, on my back, and then th[…]other one, I was no longer sure, was g[…]ry snake eating the buttons on my shi[…]

I lost t[…]nvolved, whether it was five, or ten, or[…] that illuminated Fiona's face. I left M[…]one on the mauve seat in Barcelon[…]d out and counted each of his teeth wi[…]

"Yo[…]ted to ask him.

"Wh[…]" he said.

I re[…]here I was and the purpose of what […]he'd kissed me. John looked at me. H[…] backed up a bit to better focus on hi[…] and honest look. I felt that this was […]ssed my cheeks with the same soft[…]er microphone in my now hazy mer[…]

"[…]ow."

[…]" he said as if he had always known it.

I grabbed his face and returned his lips to my neck. I tilted my face and raised my chin to leave him ample room and John resumed

Sinopsis: André vive en su zona de confort hasta que conoce a la elegante Michele, veinticinco años mayor que él. El día en que ella visita el prestigioso viñedo donde él trabaja, comienza una historia difícil y repleta de contradicciones, pero al mismo tiempo llena de ternura, que lo llevará desde el corazón de Francia hasta Nueva York.

En la Gran Manzana, André se enfrentará a sus mayores miedos y abrirá por fin su corazón a algo que siempre se había negado.

José Soler

Licenciado en Derecho y máster en Marketing por la Universidad de Bentley, en Massachusetts. Formado en la Escuela de Escritura del Ateneu de Barcelona.

Lo nuestro no es raro es su primera novela y está inspirada en las vivencias personales del autor durante una serie de inesperados viajes por todo el mundo acompañado de una desconocida.

his kissing. "Please bite me," I asked and buried his face in my torso as I parted my knees. When he circled my nipples, I tangled my fingers in the strands of his hair. I wanted to tie myself to him in some way. John was determined to please me, but I was really looking for him to keep busy so that he couldn't see my face get emotional at his wonderful declaration of love. I wanted to enjoy it alone, in my own world. The certainty of love, nothing more and nothing less. Wasn't that what he'd just said?

"Would you like to go upstairs?" he suggested.

"Wait," I said.

For the first time ever, he looked at me with lack of understanding, as if saying, "Why, wait for what?" Our shirts were unbuttoned, my heart was racing, the energy flowed from me to him in an inexhaustible circle, and there I was, insisting on continuing my story. Would I be testing his patience? Was I suddenly afraid again? John got up. He'd gotten a hard-on and didn't hide it. He went to get a glass of water and came back with another one for me. I had a sip. It was very cold, probably just as cold as the water I'd just thrown on him in my stubborn effort to finish my story before sleeping with him. He didn't care to know what had happened to his mother; he'd said that. Why didn't I just shut up then?

"I want to dedicate the next song to a very special couple," Fiona said. "They know who they are."

Two of the couples looked at each other with complicity, the others with boredom, and once again I had the feeling that Michele and I had become Fiona's scapegoats that night. She had chosen each piece deliberately. She sipped a little water and smiled one by one at the audience, but once again I was left with the impression that she'd given me a more dedicated and knowing smile. When the musicians began to play the first chords of "What you won't do for love," she moved the microphone closer to her lips with an accentuated sensuality, stroked it like a lover, squinted her wonderful black eyes, and announced with the solemnity of great occasions that the dance floor was formally open. The ostrich family came out en masse. The parents had no sense of rhythm and neither did the children. They danced as if the music being played was the twist, waving their arms and legs ostentatiously. The kids imitated the parents but at least they kept their limbs attached to their bodies. Occasionally, the four of them got into a huddle, grabbing each other by the forearms, and jumped uninhibited. They were having a great time and couldn't care less about the others. I also had a family one day to dance and laugh with, and to hug. I remembered the open-air dance on the Costa Brava, in that hotel among the pine trees with the pool carved into the rock whose name I could possibly recall if it did me any good. Samantha and I boogied, hopefully more gracefully than the ostrich family, while Christine, very young then, clung to my leg like a koala totally determined to keep it on the ground. They were happy times, now long gone.

Next, an older couple who walked very stiffly joined them. They reached the dance floor holding hands and began to dance slowly, cheek to cheek, immune to the ostrich family pirouettes. They danced in their own couple of square feet as if they had all the time in the world. They'd probably danced in the same way their entire lives, at every ceremony, at each party, at their silver anniversary and, who knows, maybe their golden one too. They looked at each other from time to time with that pride of having made it together to that night. I felt an unhealthy prick of envy. Michele pretended to be distracted, tapping the table to the rhythm of the music.

"I love this song," she said. She sipped her cava and challenged me with her blue gaze. She had a hard time hiding that she was dying to dance with me.

Two men, obviously a couple, also brought themselves to the dance floor. They didn't dance close, but their eyes never left each other except when the one with the bow tie spun around, then waved his arms as if he were playing the maracas and went back to his partner just in time not to miss the new arrivals.

A silver-templed couple—he very tall and she very short—were determined to show that they were more agile and gifted than the other old couple, like some Fred Astaire and Ginger Rogers wannabes. I also wanted to dance. My knees pointed to the dance floor, which was as lively as it was going to be that night. It was now or never.

If we both wanted to dance, what was the problem?

Michele deserved a dance. A public one, in broad daylight. I had to prove to her that I loved her despite what other people might think, beyond our age difference, social class convention, or my own sexual identity. Yes, Michele deserved recognition for always remaining by my side, even at the times when I hadn't treated her fairly; backing me up in absolutely everything; and loving me as I was—although I'd kept her from really knowing me. I thought I'd just say, "Mrs. Jones?" and let cava and Fiona's lullabies do the rest. I thought many things that I didn't do, and I let the party dissolve like the cream in a coffee, and therefore the occasion passed. Ostrich mom retired before the song ended with an "I am exhausted" face. The kids followed her, and the father also quit dancing after giving them a helpless look.

"You don't like this song?" Michele said. The opportunity was still there. I was still in time to not disappoint her.

"Oh, it's beautiful," I said, and did nothing but look how Michele's excitement vanished. She lowered her eyelids to avoid direct eye contact, as if she were, as she should be, disenchanted with me.

I had been a coward once more, I thought as the gay couple passed by my side on their way back to their table. On the dance floor, the oldest couple continued to display their love story, while Fred and Ginger danced in circles around them. Michele looked at her watch. I looked at the ceiling.

"We won't make it," she said.

I stood up. Michele made a move to follow me, but I gestured to her to keep seated. Fiona noticed and shook her head. Had I disappointed her too? I approached the stage being careful not to disturb the four dancers. Fiona leaned down to listen to my request. She smelled of sweat and roses, of river and marsh, of dew and chocolate. She stroked my cheek and lifted her chin again.

"What did you say to her?" Michele asked when I went back.

"Wait a little, and you'll see."

Fred and Ginger stopped dancing and left the hall. They had suddenly run out of gas. A few seconds later, Fiona skipped the chorus of the song and ended it in a whisper. She didn't want to break the spell that held the two remaining dancers together. It took them a while to realize that the music had stopped. The lady opened her eyes first, looked up, then at the audience, then at herself. She covered her face with her hands, but she looked more proud than embarrassed. Her husband tried to continue dancing, but since he realized that his wife was no longer in his arms, he capitulated and kissed her on the lips. Then the audience began to applaud as if acknowledging the lifelong love they had just witnessed.

Fiona pointed to them and brought the microphone closer.

"What you won't do for love," she said, and joined the general applause, while the couple left hand-in-hand, their heads held high.

Now it was my turn, our turn. My heart started to race. Michele and I wouldn't receive as warm a reaction as the old couple. I hoped for a beautiful introduction to the song by Fiona. Why did I still care so much about what people would say?

"Ladies and gentlemen," said Fiona, taking advantage of the lingering emotion. "The next song is a special request."

All eyes focused on Michele and me. I felt them in the back of my neck. Everyone had just seen me talking to Fiona. Michele seemed calm—I'd even say happy. She pulled her hair back. She was ready for anything.

"At this moment I'm asking the French gentleman who made the request to come up to the stage and announce it himself. With his accent everything sounds more romantic."

I heard some people giggling. I was very embarrassed but couldn't back out. I loosened the knot of my tie, squeezed Michele's hand, and stood up. I greeted both sides of the room with the best smile I was capable of, and headed for Fiona, who stepped aside to make room for me.

"*Buenas noches*," I said. A couple of people answered something similar, most with a remarkable foreign accent.

Fiona walked away to say something to the musicians. I guessed she was telling them which song to play.

"I ..." I said hesitantly.

Fiona encouraged me to continue, waving her hands in the air like someone who's trying to fan a fire. Michele got up. There was a murmur.

"Is she leaving?" I thought. Quite the opposite. She started walking towards me, smiling proudly. Fiona gave me the microphone.

"May I request ..." I said with a lump in my throat.

"You may, you may," Fiona urged.

Michele was already waiting for me on the dance floor, admirably alone.

Fiona raised a finger, and the music began to play.

"Just the two of us, please," I said loudly, as my voice overlapped with the first chords of the song. I handed the microphone back to

Fiona, went down the two steps to the dance floor, and joined Michele. Fiona started singing:

"I see the crystal raindrops fall ..."

I took Michele by the waist. She responded by placing her hand on the back of my neck and moving her waist close to mine. I closed my eyes and let my imagination return to the night of our only dance prior to this one. I heard the rattle of the forest again, and the clouds passed like a herd of wildebeest in front of the African moon. The rain got my feet and her bangs wet, and we stopped caring about the world. Michele rested her cheek on my chest. Could she hear my racing heartbeat?

We started to sway.

"... Just the two of us ..." Fiona sang.

"Just the two of us," I whispered to Michele and moved my pelvis closer.

"We can make it we try," she replied.

Wrapped by Michele's arms and lulled by Fiona's silky voice in the dark theater of the Casa Fuster bar, I really thought it was possible to try. I got close to Michele's lips. She held my neck tighter and the hair on my arms stood on end. She swung her hips subtly from side to side, right to left, left to right, fanning my desire over and over again. Stirring it up. Her breathing and mine became one—quick, anxious. I was ready to kiss her right there, in front of Fiona and the musicians, under the watchful eyes of the old couple and the gay one, and before the entire ostrich family. I brought her body closer to mine, to reward her elliptical movements. I felt for the gap between her lips, tasting the waxy carmine. I felt the tip of her tongue on my tongue. It was the sweet beginning of a kiss.

And then the curtain went up. I opened my eyes. My throat dried up when I saw myself clinging to an old woman wearing emerald earrings. I stopped dancing so abruptly that Fiona had no choice but to stop singing. I let go of Michele's body. Her eyes sank in disappointment, but she kept her back straight. I looked at my hands as if I had just killed somebody and was looking for blood on them. I was afraid she would cry, although it wasn't her style to display her emotions in public. She waited a few seconds for me to say something, but I didn't.

"Was this necessary?" she whispered, and then turned to Fiona. "Your voice is a gift," she told her. She looked at me from the corner of her eye and added: "It has soul and feelings."

Then she quit the dance floor and left me alone. I saw her pick up her bag and go out the door. I looked at Fiona for the last time, hoping she would tell me what I had to do next, but she gave a look colder than Michele's. She shook her head once and then stared at the ground.

I didn't follow Michele to her room, as I considered doing. As I should have done. I needed air in my lungs and oxygen in my brain, so I headed toward the hall decisively. The doorman took off his bowler hat and opened the door for me.

"Good evening, sir," he wished me.

"Sir ..." That word reverberated. I looked up at the boy. He couldn't be more than twenty years old. His suit was too big on his shoulders, on his sleeves, in the legs. I thought of telling him that "sir" was too polite for me. It was just what I hadn't been, a gentleman. I had behaved like a teenager, like a perfect ass.

"It's a lovely evening, sir," he said smiling.

Luckily, Barcelona didn't care that I'd been a jerk in capital letters. A nice and cool breeze kissed my face the moment I stepped outside.

In front of the hotel stretched, like an outline of the Champs Elysees, the boulevard Passeig de Gracia, gently descending towards the center of the city. I took a deep breath. My eyesight wasn't sharp enough to see the end of the street. I liked Barcelona, more cosmopolitan than Strasbourg, less complicated than Paris.

Did I want to go to the heart of the city? No. I neither wanted nor surely knew how to reach the heart of anything or anyone. I wanted to run away and find a quiet place, so I turned right. Behind the hotel, the streets narrowed and were more poorly lit. I could walk in the middle of the street and talk out loud, and no one could hear me. I found comfort in being alone. To atone for my guilt, I followed the same script as usual. First, the drama: I kicked the metal shutter of a body shop. It sounded like thunder. Then the self-punishment: I called myself "asshole" a few times. Then the repentance: I had to fix what I'd done, but I didn't know how. Michele would tell me my penance. Or maybe not and that bothered me even more. She'd surely forgive me right away. Michele had an ability to love infinitely superior to mine.

"I have to go back to the hotel, talk to her, apologize," I thought at first. But then a dog happily turned the corner and stopped a second by my side. I stroked his muzzle and ears and reached down to talk to him.

"And your owner?" It licked my hands playfully. "Tell me, what's your name? Hey, what's your name?" I stroked its head. It had soft fur and smelled very good.

"Bad, bad boy," a voice said. It wasn't the dog speaking but a chubby lady dressed in black leggings and a striped Spring trench coat. She had a leash rolled around her wrist, attached to nothing. You could tell she'd been running as she was breathless. "Has he bothered you?" she asked as she hooked the leash to the dog.

I shook my head. "Not at all."

"Don't you ever run away from me again," she said to the animal. "The problem with Terriers is that they're very independent," the lady told me with a renewed smile. "Isn't that right, Boira?"

I looked one last time at the dog. He seemed resigned to his fate. I don't really know dogs, but its eyes were sadder than when it was running free, and somehow, I identified with him. Was I going to go back to the sheepfold like a baby lamb? Maybe not. My plan changed as suddenly as the wind changes direction in a storm. I knew that I had to put an end to this farce. As I retraced my steps, my goal took shape dramatically, like one of those monsters unexpectedly rising from the asphalt in a B movie. Was Michele the victim or the executioner, the fly or the spider? What exactly did I have to apologize for? For dropping everything every time she wanted to see me? Did I want to continue living this way, following Michele around the world at her every whim? What about me? Was I going to sacrifice my best years so she could enjoy her last ones to the fullest? In a matter of seconds, I went from putting my tail between my legs to sharpening my nails. The latent rivalry that had always existed between us became, ipso facto, a kind of enmity. My relationship with Michele had to change radically and immediately. I wish—but I didn't think like this until later—that I had counted to ten and reflected more on my thoughts, especially knowing that I am a man of extremes. Things would have ended differently. But at that time there was no turning back. I sped up. I had a mission to accomplish, a rival to stop admiring, an enemy to defeat. I entered the hotel lobby without waiting for the doorman to welcome me. I climbed the stairs to the fourth floor. Michele's door was at the end of the hall.

"The door was dark blue, almost black," I said to John.

"Can I ask you something?" he said. I liked that he asked me for permission before asking certain questions. I was much more thoughtless.

"Of course. Anything you want."

"Why did you want to reopen a door you had just decided to close? Not very elegantly, by the way. Why did you go back to her room?"

Isn't that what I always did? Go back to her?

"Good question. I don't know."

"You should be more consistent. I'm under the impression that you are doing the same with me. Backing off."

Hearing the truth can hurt, especially when coming from someone you care about.

"But I'm not going to let you do that, no way," John smiled.

"I am sorry."

"Are you telling *me* or did you ask Michele for forgiveness?" John said, relaxing his eyebrows. He grabbed my hand and gave me my opening again: "The door was blue ..."

I was about to knock on her door when I realized that it was ajar. Michele knew I'd be coming. I still knocked on it softly.

"Come in," she said in a neutral tone of voice.

I did. The dim light gave the room the sepia effect of an old photo. Michele was sitting on the edge of the bed, her legs crossed, no stockings, barefoot. She was reading something on her cell phone.

"Big trouble in the Middle East," she said without looking up.

"We need to talk," I said, taking a step forward. I stayed next to the armoire. A gold ring and the emerald earrings rested on top of its wooden surface.

"Go ahead then."

She looked at me with a blank, unhurried face. I took the ring.

"Is this your wedding ring?" I asked.

"It's a little loose. I need to have it fixed."

"How come you still wear it?"

"Becoming a widow was not my decision." I left it on the table again. I took another step. "I guess in my own way I keep my promises," she added, uncrossing her legs.

"You and your ways."

"And you and yours, honey, which are not always the best."

"I didn't behave well today," I said, immediately regretting my childish tone. If I kept on like that, I'd soon be on her leash again.

"Certainly not. You have to ask yourself what drives you to behave like this; where that rage comes from."

"I already know the answer."

"Which is?"

"The situation, us, all this is ridiculous."

Michele turned her head to the side, as if I'd slapped her, but she immediately looked at me defiantly, a lock of hair over one eye.

"You kissed me," she said.

"This is not going anywhere," I said.

"It won't go anywhere we don't want it to go. *We* won't go where *we* do not want to go."

"Relationships either evolve or die. You said that, remember?"

"Sit down."

"I'm fine standing, thanks."

Michele got up. We were now both standing.

"You are so tall, André." We were three steps away and yet a world apart. In the back of the room, behind the half-drawn curtains, I smelled freedom. "You have already made me feel small enough today," she said.

I passed by her side and sat on the bed.

"Happy?" Now she was higher up.

"I had never looked at you as a man but today ..."

I didn't believe a word of what she was telling me. From day one, and on each trip, she had pushed for a growing intimacy. She'd always gone a little further than was conventionally acceptable. However, given the circumstances, I chose not to accuse her of being a liar.

"Today what?" I asked.

"When you took me by the waist ... I was turned on."

I laughed. I wasn't expecting her comment, but it somehow spoke to our shared memories, so I wished that we could laugh at it together.

"Really?" I said, only somewhat incredulous.

"You don't understand."

I did. I'd felt the same sometimes, that strange mixture of excitement and rejection. The difference was that I'd never admit that in front of her. Michele was way more honest.

"At a certain age, women become invisible. No one looks at us."

"I see." I was not willing to let her play the pity card.

"On the dance floor you made me feel alive. I wasn't see-through, do you understand? They were watching me, not my emeralds."

"Michele ..."

"Wait! Let me finish. I only existed because I had you by my side." She came to sit on the bed. She pulled the lock of hair away from her face and stroked my cheek. "You give me life," she said.

I pulled my head back. Michele's proximity bothered me and at the same time turned me on.

"I don't want to have that responsibility," I said. I was starting to feel weak. I had come to finish with the relationship, not to save it. If she got me to feel guilty, I'd never put an end to it.

"You must have felt something as well to kiss me." I closed my eyes for a moment to relive the sensation of the brief contact of our tongues and the enticing movement of her pelvis, a movement like the infinity sign that Fiona had drawn in the air at the beginning of the concert.

Unexpectedly, Michele placed a kiss on my lips:

"I love you."

I swept her kiss to the inside of my mouth. It tasted complex like a good brandy.

"This is just what I don't need," I said.

I didn't want to open my eyes as I had done onstage. I didn't want to see the furrows of time in Michele's face.

"Shh," she whispered. "Don't think."

I was about to succumb. Don't think. Don't talk. She would think for both of us. She'd fill my head with beautiful words so there would be no room for my own. I got the message. I just had to be. Be by her side, always. Chained to her. I just didn't want to. I pulled away.

"It's not enough," I said.

"What?" she said, surprised.

"Your love, that you love me, it's not enough."

I got up and headed towards the door. Before leaving, I turned around. I was sad to see her, so small on that big bed. No shoes. No stockings. No jewelry. No future.

"I don't want to sound ungrateful," I said, "but you forget that I also have to love you. Love requires two."

I would never see Michele again, but I talked to her once a little later. "At that conversation," I told John, "it's when she told me about you."

"What a jerk you were, forgive me for telling you," John interrupted. Coming from him, always so restrained, it was food for thought. It was the first time a bad word had come out of his mouth despite the loving tone he'd disguised it with. He was right. That certainly hadn't been the classiest way to put an end to such an important relationship.

"Do you think?" I liked that he gave me a good talking-to, that he stood up to an injustice, even when I had been the offender.

"What I think is that you have to give people the chance to find out about your flaws little by little and by themselves. It doesn't help you to point them out. Quite the opposite, it works against you."

"I was fed up, John. Sick of her."

"*You* turned her on," he continued slowly. "When they do it to us, that has a name. You humiliated her in public and then in private. And, on top of that, you allowed yourself the luxury of leaving her. You were fed up, you say? Of what?"

He let go of my hand and posed the big question:

"Is that who you are?"

He got up and went to get something from the dresser. He turned his back on me.

"You're being a little tough on me," I said, although I didn't believe it at all. John had set the issue down in black and white.

"Tell me," he said as he searched through a drawer. "Why are you telling me all this? It seems to me that all this has little to do with this operetta of yours with Michele. For some reason, and don't ask me why, it's as if you wanted me to see you as a bad person, like you want to punish yourself or something."

He came back with a small metal box and sat down next to me. He rested it on his knees and took my hands. Then he squeezed them tightly. Although John had raised the tone of his voice considerably, I felt more secure than ever.

"Love yourself, André! Stop going around referring to the times you've behaved like a jackass. I don't see that ungrateful person at all when I look at you, and surely neither did Michele. Do you know what I see? A man who is a little lost."

"Are you telling me that I need help?"

"Love is what you need. Like everyone, like me."

"Great," I said, smiling. "What a sexy way to introduce myself! As someone needy, instead of as an imaginative, resourceful person. I'm so pathetic."

He squeezed my hands again.

"Do you know that I love your smile? No one with a smile like yours can be bad." He came over and kissed me. He tasted of apples and blooming flowers. He opened the box. "Do you smoke?"

I hadn't smoked a joint since high school. While he was rolling it, I continued telling him my version of what had happened after I left Michele's room.

When I returned to my room, I knew she would call me, but I thought she'd do it sooner. She let more than half an hour go by. In that time, I totally imagined her deciding point by point what she was going to say. I also knew she'd wait for me to call her first, but I was determined to stand my ground. My emotional dependence on Michele had become detrimental to my well-being and prevented me from progressing. Michele was the main obstacle on my road to happiness. When the telephone finally rang, I waited until the third ring before answering. I even considered not picking it up at all.

"Hello?"

Michele didn't respond right away.

"Is this a farewell?" she finally asked me.

"It doesn't have to be forever. But I need some time."

"I don't have time, André," she replied impatiently. Now I realize the true extent of her haste.

"It's my fault," she said, "for kissing you, for trying to take it further."

She had to be very desperate to accept the responsibility. It was not typical of her.

"It is nobody's fault." I didn't want to crush her anymore. I had humiliated her enough.

"What do you need?" she asked.

"Nothing you can give me."

"Try me."

"Time," I insisted, but my first impulse was to say, "a good cock."

"Don't ask me for time."

"I need to find myself."

"And I don't let you?"

"You said it."

"But I want you to be happy."

"Again with the same."

She paused to mark a turn in the conversation.

"If we are not going to talk anymore, then I have to tell you something. Something that nobody knows."

Dredging up at that moment a secret would get me more involved in her life when I wanted exactly the opposite. I was not surprised. Michele always added more fuel to the fire when she thought the flame was dying out. She would never let me go. Ever.

"What for, Michele? To show me that only you know the true value of friendship?"

"Can you come to my room?"

"No."

"Can I go to yours?"

"Neither!"

I couldn't let her put me on her leash again. If I met with Michele, one way or another she'd manage to convince me of the benefits of our relationship, and it would be a never-ending story. She would tell me everything I wanted to hear. She would remind me how unique our "thing" was. She would suffocate me with the smell of roses of impossible colors.

"You are being unfair," she said.

That hurt me. I considered myself a fair man. Michele did not take a second to add:

"At least listen to me."

"I *am* listening to you. Am I not listening to you?"

"What did I do to you? Why are you angry? I want to understand you."

I tried to answer myself these questions fairly, which showed that Michele's strategy was working. I began to analyze the situation from her point of view. In good conscience, I couldn't accuse her of having done anything to me, at least not that night. If she had done nothing, my anger was just a tantrum, which I was convinced was not the case.

"It's not about you, it's about me," I said. Michele would have a hard time refuting what I felt. In a more favorable context to her, she would have answered something like, "Only you can assess if it's worth it to you," but this time she couldn't risk putting the decision in my hands. I would have told her "Goodbye."

"I need to understand what worries you."

As always, she wanted to go deeper, and I wanted to end the conversation. Her solution was *more Michele*. I needed the opposite.

"It's too bad that I don't feel the need to tell you."

"Why do you always wear armor?"

This question was a classic, so I kept waiting for the next one.

"I don't deserve it," she said.

If I didn't reverse the situation, soon the indignant person would be Michele, and I'd find myself consoling her.

"I'm leaving tomorrow," I said.

"Oh my God, André," John told me as he carefully finished rolling the joint. "Are you listening to yourself?"

I stopped cold.

"You're almost getting me to love Michele. Don't you have feelings?"

"You had to live through it," I replied. John gave me the opportunity to look back at the situation with the perspective of time and from a different place. Michele was not an ogre—he was right. There was no better friend, no one more suffocatingly committed to my happiness.

"Make love, not war, André," he smiled.

"I suppose that with her the problem was to get the dose right. I still haven't told you when and why she told me about you."

"Have I asked you?" He swung the joint in the air to make sure it was perfectly straight. It looked like a Marlboro. It was perfect, but John twisted his mouth a little, as if he were not entirely satisfied with the result.

"Do you want to know?"

"Honestly? I've already told you before that I don't. But if you're going to feel better, just go ahead. I'll listen to you."

"I'll be compassionate and spare you the details, but I'm glad she told me about you. Meeting you is the best thing that has happened to me lately." John smiled. "Besides, if you have forgiven her ..."

"I did not say that. I simply don't want to resurrect the dead."

"Me neither," I replied.

"Come on, join me outside for a smoke. I like it before." He winked at me and showed me his cute fangs, and I felt again the pulse in my crotch. "Then I'll show you how we do it in Chatham." He got up from the sofa. He leaned down, tickled me on the left side and held out his arm to help me stand up. His arm was hard and strong. We kissed. We looked at each other. He smiled at me. I hugged him. We kissed again, looked at each other again and laughed. We were both sure of what we wanted. I followed him to the back porch behind the kitchen. Before leaving, I touched his ass. It was round and tight. Divine. Smoking now? What a waste of time.

Maybe one day I'll tell him the truth. Maybe I'll tell him that I had to pick up my underwear from the floor before leaving room 409 at the Casa Fuster and admit that I gave Michele the speech about love requiring two people with my shoes in one hand and my socks in the other. Maybe. But very likely I won't say anything to John just like I never told Michele that I'm gay. Why tell him if he doesn't really care anyway? In the end, I told him something much more important. I told him the humiliating way that I treated Michele and how I paid back her love. I hope he accepts me as I am. I've got my hopes up about him.

While we were going out the door that led to the courtyard, I had my mind on other things. I had resurrected the fantasy of what John's room would look like—would it have mosquito netting?—and had resigned myself to accepting that break to smoke marijuana as a kind of purgatory. It was only fair that John now set the pace and made me wait to savor the sweetness of sex. Quid pro quo. Tit for tat.

The courtyard was dark. I hadn't seen it before, but it felt vaguely familiar. The sky, stained here and there with milk chocolate clouds, showed through the treetops. The stars shone where it was clear. I felt the breeze on my face, on my chest, slipping to the sides, down my unbuttoned shirt. It was cool out there. The back porch was narrower than the one in the front, with only one rickety chair in a corner. The light on the ceiling was off. John sat down at the top of the steps and invited me to sit next to him. The steps led down to a spacious patio, longer than it was wide, and mostly paved. At the end, there was a casita or some sort of garage with a large door and a basketball hoop on the wall. In the dim light I could not tell the color. At night all cats are gray. I imagined John playing there as a child. He probably had lots of friends in the neighborhood. That humble structure may have witnessed his first kisses. Would they have been with a boy or with a girl? I remembered my first sexual games. I couldn't help but smile.

John put the cigarette to his lips. Few people could perform that ritual with his elegance. He took a lighter out. He looked like an English lord about to light his pipe.

"I have another one somewhere," he said when his lighter didn't work.

He went back into the house and left me staring into the darkness of the courtyard. You couldn't hear anything. This was certainly a neighborhood for lovers of tranquility. Where were the dogs? I thought I'd ask him when he came back.

I decided to stretch my legs. I was cold. I went down the steps and walked slowly in the direction of the mysterious building, about fifty yards away. As I got closer, I started to have the strange feeling that I had already been here. Impossible. I had seen a little bit of the garden on the other side, but not the patio. I looked back. The kitchen light reflected some light on the patio. I could see my shadow, but not much more. I looked at the sky. There was no sign of the moon. That's why the stars shone so brightly.

I was halfway there when I found that the building was a garage and neither gray nor brown, but a cream color. I had a hunch, a premonition, that tingling of the nerves before making a discovery. Then John came out, and this time he turned on the light. Both the porch and the outside of the garage lit up, revealing the garage's true color:

Yellow.

In a hallucination, I saw the boy with the knowing smile on Michele's photo riding on his bike. He was pedaling at full speed toward me. He stopped at my feet, at the door of the yellow house. He blew his bangs off his eyes, looked at me with an intrigued gaze, and then his image froze forever on photographic paper.

I finally understood. Everything fit. The boy on the Polaroid was John as a child. Dawson and John were two sides of the same coin. The photo had been taken here, many years ago, perhaps by Michele herself. As John suspected, she had tracked him throughout his life. That's why he had always noticed her presence. Michele was everywhere. It was useless to run away from her.

"Are you coming?" John said in a very sexy voice.

I debated between telling him about what I had discovered right then, which seemed the most honest choice, what the mind asked me to do, or tell him later. Mind, reason, logic, principles. To hell with them! This time I'd do what my body told me. I'd follow my instincts. I didn't want to wait any longer to have John in my arms, to kiss him and bite his boxers off, to lick his entire body and become one. I didn't want to wait any longer to fly away, as Michele had asked me, or to flow, like Bernadette encouraged me to do. To live a full life. With that in mind, I started back to the porch, where John was waiting for me. I took the cigarette from his hands and took a drag. I felt the hot smoke go down my throat and made a great effort not to cough. I kept it in my lungs for a few seconds and then blew it on the bit of air, light and sparse, between us. I laughed—it was one of those silly laughs—and John sealed it with a kiss which didn't permit any further delay. I threw the butt on the ground, and we went back in.

"Remind me to tell you something," I said without remorse as we went up the stairs to his bedroom.

"Shh. Tell me later."

THURSDAY

When I opened my eyes, the day had already dawned, and the sun was coming in shyly through the window. John was lying next to me, his cheek resting on the palm of his hand. He looked at me. I had the feeling that he'd been like that for a long time, my thinking man. I rubbed my feet against his. They were cold. He caressed my butt. "Good morning, handsome," he whispered and gave me one of his smiles. I closed my eyes again, but John's light had already awakened me. I stretched my arms and legs. I arched my spine.

"What a good way to wake up," I said.

John ran a finger from my navel to my chin. I bit it tenderly. I would have eaten it. In his skin I recognized my own smell and a new one of spilled night and fresh dawn.

"I'm going to be late," he said.

"Call and say you're sick."

To help him with his decision, I pulled the sheet over our heads. The temperature was rising rapidly in that makeshift world of ours, so small and magical. I pressed my body to his, and I kissed him:

"Stay with me today, please. It's my last day."

John responded well to the closeness of my skin. My kiss multiplied on his lips. One miracle turned into another while outside the morning bloomed.

"I wish I could, but I have to go to work." I kept kissing him. "Close the month, balance the books ..."

He dragged his heels. He ran his legs between my calves. I felt his flesh. I wasn't happy with the idea of not spending that Thursday together or at least the first few hours of it. I was leaving the next day. I held on tightly to the hope he wouldn't leave. His desire not to leave grew and so did my desire for him to stay, and when both were huge and his feet were warm like mine, I reached out to the table and handed him the phone.

"Tell them the truth, that you have a sudden fever."

John didn't go to work, although his temperature dropped as soon as I applied my first aid. We had all day ahead of us, and it was time to decide what to do with those precious hours. I had liked the Frick Museum so much that John suggested another small one called The Cloisters that could be reached by subway.

"How do you know that I will like it?"

"I just know."

The place was very strange but lived up to its name. It was made up of a series of medieval structures and cloisters as if it were a church, with a Romanesque tower that dominated the complex. The Cloisters was located in the middle of a park in the upper part of Manhattan, on a cliff that overlooked the Hudson River. As soon as we left the station, I had the feeling that we were hundreds of miles away from the heart of New York. From the museum you couldn't see any other buildings, and the views were unobstructed. John explained to me that Rockefeller had brought all these stones, one by one, from different parts of Europe.

"Most came from France. And as you can see, they have acclimated well," he said mischievously. I doubted whether he'd just planted a seed, Michele's style, or maybe I was reading into his remark more than there was.

Once inside, we found ourselves surrounded by a series of tapestries called *The Hunting of the Unicorn.*

"You won't believe this," I said to John, "but on a recent trip to Paris I saw a very similar unicorn set. There were six of them, if I remember correctly."

"Then one has escaped Paris and has come to New York. Here there are seven."

"I can see you are a great accountant," I joked. "Each tapestry represented a sense, plus a very mysterious sixth one called 'À Mon Seul Desir,' something like 'My Only Desire.'" Driven by desire I kissed him when the guard turned around, and I whispered in his ear, "Do you know what I think of whenever I see a unicorn?"

I liked talking to John, even about fantastic beings. If I had been alone in that room, I wouldn't have spent more than five minutes there, but he made me look at those tapestries with new eyes, those of an artist. He explained to me the artist's tricks to convey the violence in the hunt for the beast. He drew diagonals where I had not seen them. I had no idea of the tension a simple oblique line could bring. What did I know of diagonals or perspective? I liked museums but as a simple amateur. Just by raising or lowering the horizon line he made me feel big or small, important or superfluous. More knowledge to add to his theory of the blobs of paint.

"Do you realize that we are wasting our time with some animals that don't exist?" I asked.

John looked surprised.

"Then I must be blind and you too because these walls are full of unicorns, and there are more in Paris, according to you. So they not only exist, but they run all over the world."

I smiled. He was a worthy son of Michele, but I didn't dare to tell him that.

He grabbed my hand. It seemed so normal and, at the same time, so extraordinary.

"At our desire," I said.

"A *notre seul désir*. How did I say it?"

He'd said it so-so, but with that sexy voice that spoke directly to the sixth sense that drives me to him.

I was sorry to say goodbye to John in the subway and to do it in such a poor way—with a handshake and a hurried hug just before getting off the subway alerted by the warning beep of the closing doors. Although it was an *au revoir* and not an *adieu,* I almost didn't get off but stayed with him to Penn, and then to Chatham, and then who knows, but my last night was for Lucy. On Broadway.

I sent him a kiss from the platform while the train started to move. I wanted to tell him, "I love you," but I held back. Too much, too soon. It wasn't my style.

I walked from the subway to Lucy's more slowly than usual. I was leaving the next day—yesterday—and I wanted to record in my memory bank the neighborhood's images and smells. Its soundtrack. I took pictures of silly things, like Geppetto's neon sign—which was turned off because it wasn't even 5:00 pm—and of the pizza in the window, even if it looked a little dry. I also took photos of the dried gum on the sidewalk, of an old woman with a toothless yet beautiful smile, and of the boring, milky sky. I shot a video of the traffic with the yellow cabs, where you can hear a madman call me "motherfucker," then "brother" and then ask me for money for beer. I took a selfie in front of the flower shop before going in to get Lucy a rose.

"I got you a little something too," she told me when I gave it to her. She opened a kitchen drawer and pulled out an irregular, roughly wrapped package.

"Be careful when you open it, you could hurt yourself."

I couldn't help letting out a loud laugh when I unwrapped it.

"I just had to buy it for you. Isn't it just like the one on your shirt, with the two limbs and all?" she said, laughing.

Lucy was hilarious. That girl had given me a cactus.

FRIDAY

Friday. It's only been nine days since I received Michele's letter. Lucy's laugh is mixed with the multiple "Hello" from *The Book of Mormon*'s first act, which still resonate in my head. What a great night. I can't believe it was yesterday, and all this just happened to me: Lucy's farewell, falling in love with John, my one-night stand with Tony, the "Dawson mystery," the news of Michele's death. This is movie material, maybe a tragicomedy.

The cactus has stayed in New York, of course, but I did bring the best of Lucy back to France. Her optimism and sense of humor. The good vibes she gives off. Her friendship. Although Lucy has not been the main character of this story, for me she is already a star. I hope that the results of her tests clear the ghost of cancer and that her light continues to glow with the same golden sparks as it did that night at the Pink, when the glitter shone on her neck, and she looked so beautiful and full of life. We'll know in a few days. Until Tuesday, Lucy can only wait. As for Michele, I still have one thing to do for her. It will be tomorrow. Today I am tired after the long trip. I hope that I get inspired in my sleep. I am neither a writer nor a poet.

SATURDAY

Dear Michele,

I came back from New York yesterday. I unpacked and did some laundry. I talked to Christine. I really can't wait to see her. She reminded me to bring the Nikes that I got her at Foot Locker when I see her in Paris next month—I'll tell you later what that trip is about—and of course, I read your letter again. In light of what I know now, it was as if I were reading it for the first time. By the way, I spilled some wine, and the ink ran. I smiled when that happened. Of all the grievances, this is the one you'd be quickest to forgive. Our wine. We've shared a few bottles all over the world! In France, in Argentina, and at the tip of Africa. It was a Côtes du Rhone, nothing very glamorous. I'll try to spill a Chateauneuf du Pape next time. Take my clumsiness as our last drink together, will you?

Do you know that John is a lot like you? He's intelligent and persevering. Hopefully, he'll even grow to love me like you did, and I will love him too. We've decided to try to make it work, despite the distance. New York is not exactly around the corner. He'll be coming in a few weeks. We'll meet in Paris. Paris is beautiful in Summer. Can you believe that he has never been to Europe? I'll take the chance and go see Christine too before she leaves for Amsterdam. These kids don't stop. I'll send John to the Louvre, or better, to the Cluny, so he can entertain himself with his beloved unicorns. I'm not ready to come out of the closet with Christine yet, although she's probably figured it out already. One step at a time.

And you, when did you know? I have the feeling that since the beginning, from day one. Maginot. Now I see that name everywhere, just like when Samantha was pregnant, and we saw expectant women all over the place, but when you mentioned it for the first time it sounded like a distant echo from my history books. You'll be glad to know that my Maginot Line is a bit weaker today than when you met me. At times, it's a dashed line. You should have seen me in New York. I was like you in your best times!

It seems to me that my lack of interest in ladies was quite clear at that dinner with Carol. Even she noticed. And, although I don't think it showed too much—I hope—there were all the other signs, right? If you still had any doubts you had your confirmation in Barcelona. Remember. I left your room crestfallen, with my shoes in one hand and my socks in the other, like a broken toy. I was so ashamed that I could not consummate what we'd begun that I was unable to see you again. Everything else could be fixed. Forgive me, you didn't deserve it.

With John, I refer to you as Michele, never "your mother." I know he hates that I talk about you, but at least now he tolerates it. If our relationship works, I'll try to change his mind regarding you. He still holds a grudge. It will take time, but now you have all the time in the world. Leave it in my hands.

John listens to me. I think he understands me. And he kisses well. He does everything well, so tenderly and decisively. He's attentive and affectionate. A true love. It's too soon to know where this will end, but I like him. I like him a lot. Didn't you say, "Go see John. He should know that he is not alone in this world"? Only today did I understand, in re-reading your letter, that you were referring to me. I was that person you wanted for John. I'd been shooting in the dark believing you were talking about Dawson, and it turns out Dawson is a stupid town in North Dakota. By the way, neither one of us understand this mess very well. Why would I care whether you had a natural child, or two, or twenty? But as John pointed out: why would it matter to you that I was gay? As you can see, he's also wise, just like his mother. I can call you that. You see how silly I was; how absurd everything was. We would have loved each other just the same, probably more. Let's call it a draw if you don't mind. Do me this last favor.

There has to be much more in this whole Dawson affair for John and I to figure out. You had to have some powerful reason to create this fictional son. We lack information. And, believe me, we really chewed on that at The Cloisters. God, it was the day before yesterday, and I already miss John. I told him that pain can compel us to make up a kinder story. It's tempting to replace what we did with what we wished we'd done. The difficult thing is to tell the first lie, or as in my case, not to tell the whole truth to begin with. Besides, back then you'd just met me, and we weren't supposed to see each other again, so you decided to be who you wanted to be. And you were. You were the mother that you couldn't or weren't allowed to be. Who doesn't build useless barriers at some point and lock himself inside? Who doesn't draw his own Maginot Line? I know that the essential truth, your feelings towards me, were genuine. That's more than enough for me.

Today I had a dream, or rather a thought, because I was already awake but in that first hour of tossing and turning when one doesn't know yet what time it is. I was in San Francisco, under that sky that we will no longer see together. Of all places, I found myself sitting on the roots of the maple tree that grows on the lonely patch of grass on top of Vallejo Street. It was all as you described it in your letter: the yellow trash bin, the wooden bench, the names of the lovers etched with a knife in the maple's bark and on the slats of the bench. The fog clung to the hill and hid the sea. It is true, my love, that the ocean is far below. You were chatting with a nanny. The girl listened to you and nibbled on her sandwich. I knew you were telling her the whole story, including the gaps that drive John and I crazy, but as much as I tried to hear what you said, your words died in the air. I couldn't hear you, and you couldn't see me. Does that sound familiar? At one point, the nanny got up, shook the crumbs from her jeans and left. Then I ran to sit next to you. You seemed so real that I thought I was the ghost. I held out my hands to you with my palms up, and you looked at them with nostalgia, almost with envy. You smiled, as you always did when you saw me, and in the blue of your eyes I saw a bit of the sea wedged in the fog. An impossible reflection, we know that. I held your hands. They were bonier than the last time in Barcelona. You told me that you did not expect me so soon. I replied that this time you had surpassed yourself. Your smile got wider.

"You think?" you answered. As if you didn't know what you had done! Then you shivered. "It's starting to get cold; the fog is rising."

"One day John will understand that you loved him. I'll make him understand," I told you while your eyes turned gray.

"Leave before you are caught in the fog."

I talked faster. I knew time was running out.

"You knew him; you knew me; you arranged that we met. If our story has a happy ending one day, like I wish, it will be thanks to you."

"Don't be silly, André. Thanks to you for coming. I thought I would not see you again."

Before you faded away, you told me with a loving sigh:

"Be happy. Enjoy life. Fly away!"

Forever yours,

André

P.S: Halfeti's mailman will go crazy trying to find Black Roses Avenue.

ABOUT THE AUTHOR

José Soler (Barcelona, Spain, 1971) studied Law in his hometown. In his late twenties, he moved to Boston and earned his master's degree in Marketing from Bentley College. He then moved back to Spain and founded Pepito Tours, a company specializing in private tours of Barcelona. As a tour guide, he began telling stories and hasn't stopped since. "It Wasn't So Strange After All" is his first novel, originally published in Spanish as "Lo Nuestro No Es Raro" by Penguin Random House.

You can follow José on Instagram: @josesolerfraile

Printed in Poland
by Amazon Fulfillment
Poland Sp. z o.o., Wrocław

79742745R00132